Chief's Café, Amsterdam

Mithun B. Nasrin

i

First published in Great Britain as a softback original in 2017

Typeset in Dante MT Std

Editing, typesetting and publishing by UK Book Publishing
www.ukbookpublishing.com

Cover artist: Sorno Monjuri Zaman

ISBN: 978-1-912183-11-1

This book is dedicated to

Dr. Lisette Luykx

Dearest of all

Thanks

I was born into a cosmopolitan family. Throughout the years I have come across many people and most of them have left a large imprint on my mind. Thanking someone on a book page does not feel the same as remaining thankful to the person in reality. A large life also contains a large group of people from different places and to some of them I am especially grateful.

A large life brings with it fun as well as difficulties, and others who care about me can feel this too. So one day, while I was not feeling like my usual self, I received an e-mail from my dear friend Ella de Voogd from the Netherlands. Being a great diplomat, she wrote in a diplomatic way that it is better to start writing something than just sitting and feeling miserable. A huge thanks to Ella for sending that piece of advice. I guess it is always good to listen to a diplomat.

On the 12th of December 2016, I went upstairs to my atelier and opened Dulce (my ten-year old white laptop and faithful companion) and said to her, 'Girl, we must do something.' She smiled and said, 'Why don't we talk with our poet?' She meant Chekote Washakey, the poet, singer and composer, who knows every brick of the city of Amsterdam and who is full of vibrant stories about the city. Chekote is a natural storyteller and has been telling us stories to fill our ears and hearts. I must thank him for first giving me the idea of writing about Amsterdam, which is his loving home.

I thank my family for being around me and taking care of me. Most of all I am grateful to my sister Mrs Ashfia Yahya, who is a universal mother figure. Her mother-like love and affection has kept me going for many years now. Thank you, Apa.

Special thanks to Mr M. Mohsinul Hoque, the judge, for being around me as a little brother and helping me every which way needed.

I also thank Ms Sorno Monjori Zaman (Moyna), the aspiring doctor, for drawing the cover design. And William, who has never failed to bring me a cup of tea with a piece of Dutch bread, sent from the Netherlands by our great friend Jan Schrijvers. Thanks for the life-saving parcels, Jan. A huge thanks also to a very dear friend, Hein Berkhout, for writing loving letters and sending hope and courage.

I also have to mention Monique van Hinte, without whom the Amsterdam mime school would have been no fun. What good times we used to have biking in Amsterdam, with Monique doing the biking and me sitting on the carrier at the back. Thanks, dear Monique, for those uncomplicated lovely days. Thanks to Merel van Gaalen, a writer and actress, who has been a great friend for many years. The same warm thanks to Sinta Hutahaen, the Indonesian engineer lady, who was great fun at the English department as a student. While we were all failing the syntax exams, like an epidemic, making our teacher profoundly unhappy, she passed, without us! What audacity!

Thank you, Sinta, for remaining a friend for so many years.

At one point in the writing, I was searching and searching for a word for a particular part of a piano and even Google could not help me! I mailed my friend Annemarie van Woerkom, a great pianist, and she sent me the word immediately. Thank you, Annemarie, for the 'hydro-cell bar'.

When my previous novel 'The Smell of Home' was published in 2016 by Austin Macauley Publishers, one of the questions they asked for their promotional material was, 'Who would you like to meet very much?' The name that straightaway popped up in my mind was, 'Noam Chomsky'. As they say, when you want something very badly, you get it. I had been wanting to meet him for a very long time, to tell him how his old student at MIT, Dr Rudolf de Rijk, had enriched my mind by discussing Chomskyan ideas with me. I had been thinking I should somehow convey to Professor Chomsky that my dearest friend Rudolf is not with us anymore. Suddenly, in May of this year in Reading, I found myself shaking hands with Chomsky and sitting next to him, talking about Rudolf's Basque grammar book and his wife Virginia's Thanksgiving turkey wings. I met the real man Chomsky, who was not the towering figure of linguistics, but just Noam, who could be the 'boy next-door'. Rudolf cherished Chomsky's work and would have liked to see him again. Cancer led to his untimely death but, wherever he is, Rudolf must be happy to know that I finally met Noam. I must thank Dada Rudolf for being around us for so many years and Noam for his kind smiles.

I must admit that I have been blessed in my academic life. From my primary school up to university, I have come across many fellow students and teachers. Some teachers were real gurus and some were friends. I thank them for teaching me and giving me a good time at the various universities I studied at.

After finishing this book, I immediately sent the manuscript to a publisher I knew. I was hoping the book could be published by them early in the summer of this year but their processes were slow to get going. While waiting, I met editor Ruth Lunn of UK Book Publishing and was impressed by her integrity and straightforwardness. And there and then I decided, 'This is the lady I should work with'. So I asked for my manuscript back from the other publisher. Ruth has proved herself worthy of the trust I put in her. A huge thanks to Ruth, not only for editing but for her support throughout. I thank UK Book Publishing, Consilience Media, and everyone involved in publishing my book. I also thank future readers and all those who are or will be involved in various ways with this book.

This book is the first of what will be a series, under the general title 'Chief's Café, Amsterdam'. The characters are ready for the second book. I should add that they themselves, their names and the places they visit are all imaginary. Any similarities to people, names or places outside the book are entirely coincidental.

At the end, a huge thanks to all of you and bless you all.

The author

Newcastle upon Tyne
August 2017

'My heart has become capable of every form,
It is a pasture for gazelles and a convent for
Christian monks,
And a temple for idols and the pilgrim's Ka'ba
and the Tables of the Tora and the book of the
Quran.
I follow the religion of love.'

Ibn Arabi

1

Genesis

The October sun is setting fast, lighting up the west side of the sky and spreading a fading glow over everything in this overcrowded city. Why so much haste? Why does nobody want to stop for a while and ask the fellow passers-by where they are heading and what the rush is for? And smile at them? Yes, just a little friendly smile. It would not mean much. But still it would be a smile, showing a soft face. Just a little meaningless smile to share a sense of belonging! That was the unhappy thought in her mind.

She is sitting at the top of the steps of a little staircase at street level. There are seven steps to this narrow staircase, made of grey slates, which somewhat resembles a stupa in a temple or monastery. The staircase is not really straight but built against the wall of the house, making a little landing halfway up to the first floor.

There are four floors to the houses and each is a separate little apartment, with maybe not more than forty square metres of space inside it. Well, who cares? One is more than happy to have a little island-like place like this. Not really in the sense of owning it, not really in the sense of possession. But just having the secure feeling of having a place in this city, so that one has an address of one's own.

Generally speaking, these little shoeboxes will be allotted to qualifying citizens by the housing company. Even if one is extraordinarily lucky, it will take half a lifetime to get one like this. And if anyone fancies being the owner of such a shoebox, then they have to take out a big mortgage. That mortgage will be so heavy that the weight of it will be enough to drown one in the North Sea. And on top of the monthly mortgage payments, along come the monthly service costs, which are sometimes more than the mortgage itself. One only buys a place like this to get a profit out of it.

The actual owners of these houses are not really known to their tenants, which is a blessing for both sides. The estate agent organises the lettings and takes care of them, including keeping an eye on all the awkward details, as they claim. And there is also a thing called the *'vereniging van eigenaren'*, which is the committee of the owners.

Its monthly meetings, which involve several owners, often mainly take the form of disputes and disagreements. But all the disputes are eventually settled. All the owners enjoy a democratic right to vote inside the committee. All the members may either vote or abstain from voting on a certain issue. It works like a referendum, something very much like 'Brexit'. So some of the owners have their voting rights but may choose not to vote on a particular issue.

This situation arises often, because they don't want to be impolite to a fellow owner or they do not understand the issue being voted on. But most of the time they are too tired to care. Nevertheless, coffee cups are filled up by the owner who is hosting the meeting and a closed cookie box is there on the side table, with healthy dark chocolate, some nuts, Japanese rice mix and sometimes even a piece of cashew mixed nut cake, which is always extremely delicious to be honest.

At the end of the meeting, after endless disputes,

everyone is tired and it's time to go home. Children have to be put in beds. Dogs have to be walked and the cat has to be given its supper. The owners' meetings will end with handshakes and sometimes even with three kisses on both sides of the cheeks, given with deep reluctance.

That is all part of the lives of the owners of those tiny little apartments. Maybe the bigger ones and their owners have even worse monthly meetings than these smaller ones. Certainly a larger roof creates more worries than a tiny shoebox lid. It is not easy to be the owner of an apartment in this curious city, which is in constant demand.

Still, all of them want to live there. It is not cosy. It is not particularly friendly. All those unknown faces are rushing by at volcanic speed to be on time. Yes, the appointments. One may not be late for a fraction of a second and one may not be one minute early either. Each and every one must be on time. Just on time.

The city is full of clocks. The church bells tell the time faithfully to the exact second. One knows that one has to keep time in this city. One may not be late by even one minute for an appointment. Forgiveness does not have a room in this city. Time is money and time is precious.

But she does not have to be bothered by all these rules and regulations. She does not live in one of those unaffordable pigeon holes, those island-like tiny places, where one can hide eternally, where no one cares and no-one needs to know no-one. 'Thy neighbour' here is not 'thy best friend'. It is not that one deliberately ignores one's neighbours. Not at all. The fact is that no-one has got the time or interest to know the others. But even if she had wanted to live in one of those tiny apartments, she could never have afforded it.

Instead, she works in one of the basements of those houses. Not really the basement itself but just the space behind the glass window. These windows are all the same height, about up to a tall guy's chest from street level. This is sometimes desirable for some very smart reasons. The construction gives a sense of hide and seek. It is like, you see half, and they see half.

Sometimes there are plants growing around the windows and the dark green painted window frames are often covered with climbers' branches. Sometimes a rose plant shines with orange-hue buds. Generally, one does not need to peep inside the basement. One just goes in and does what one wants to do. She gives a deep sigh again. How things have changed! Is it good? Is it bad? Does it hurt? Does it cause heartburn? Do we need so many changes around us all the time? She has a feeling that she cannot cope with all those unnecessary changes every day and everywhere.

There used to be lots of exotic shops in these rows of basements once upon a time. One could buy anything there, from a Hong Kong wig to a fresh bit of turmeric coming from the unwanted fields of Surinam. There were funny kinds of very long beans and green vegetable bananas for cooking. An old Taiwanese guy with a yellowish paper hat on his small bald head used to run a Chinese laundry, which was always very professionally done. He would thank each of his customers with huge gratitude by showing a great curtsey or making a deep bow, stooping his head pretty close to the floor. What a curious smile he had!

And then there was that homeopathic doctor from the south of Kerala. All Indians came to him for miracle drops, which were preserved in tiny little white glass bottles, tightly closed by smallish wooden corks. There were little bottles filled with alcohol. For a normal cold, he gave his patients one drop of alcohol-mixed miracle solution just on the tip of the tongue. For a severe cold, with symptoms more like pneumonia, the drops were diluted with sterile water and doubled into two. And all the patients eventually got better.

The Indian community showed great respect for their homeopathic doctor. And the Surinamese just could not do without him. His Pakistani patients went even further than that. None of them ever visited the doctor without a bowl of rice pudding or a packet of halvah in their hands. What a perfect healer he was!

Not to mention the hugely-built voodoo witch-doll maker from Zimbabwe. Yes, she was huge herself and as black as black could be. Her smooth black skin would shine under her redolent, long satin garments, which were bright red in colour and had wild birds from all over the world nested there. She used to wear a striking, huge turban, made of green and red flowery cotton, which made her head a rare piece of untouched Amazonian jungle, as if she was burdened with all sorts of exotic birds and beasts from all over our planet, as if she had been appointed a protector of wildlife.

And her large and shiny metal jingling ear rings! All ten fingers of both her hands were covered with huge rings, made of pure 23 carat gold. Everything about her was large, as large as could be. She had a large smile too, on her large two lips, her exotic, red, large lips! She had been a great help to everyone, especially that psychiatrist woman, a beautiful, tall and blonde Dutch lady, whose heart had been broken into a thousand and one pieces by an Egyptian rascal.

If one's heart is broken by an unfaithful lover, then one has every right to punish him or her for their unforgivable betrayal. One could buy a voodoo doll from her and she would give the needles for free, to prick on the heart of the doll. The betrayer would feel the same pricks on his or her heart and eventually have a heart attack, and a most unpleasant death was certain to follow afterwards.

The success of her treatment was guaranteed by her business motto. One was more than welcome to take revenge for betrayals. But there was no mention of repairing broken relationships. No, she did not care much about mending broken hearts. A broken heart will always carry a scar on it which will remain indelible. Her business was all about revenge and revenge sold very well.

But she was not all that heartless. She could tell the fortune of her clients by the sound of different kinds of drums. Her shop was full of various sorts and sizes of drums from all over the African continent and she made it clear to her customers that it was not her but her drums that carried messages from all sorts of gurus and sages from different continents to advise people on the best way of avoiding chaos in their love lives.

She hardly ever stood still. She would move around inside her shop, softly beating on the skin of the drums that were standing in every corner. Probably she was busy sending messages to the gurus and sages from all over the continents, advising her clients what to do to fall in love and how to keep their loved ones near to their hearts, so that they would not be betrayed. Now, who would not miss a person like that in one's neighbourhood and who would let her disappear just like that?

And then there was the hard working Moroccan baker with a long white beard, who had a rather protruding beer belly. It was very hard to guess his age. The very first thing he would let his customers know, with a very content and smiling face, was that he was the father of at least fifteen children.

The smell of his fresh bread would waft through the street as early as five in the morning to arouse the tummies of the sleeping souls. Early morning customers used to get a cup of Hariri soup free with their loaf of warm bread, which had been just put on the shelf straight from the oven. Her stomach starts to rumble inside her thin abdomen for a chunk of fresh bread like that.

And then there was that Pakistani Shiite imam, selling prayer rugs and incense, including the holy Islamic attar to make worship places even holier. The old rabbi of the city's biggest synagogue would be sitting in his shop and they would be talking and nodding to each other in grave agreement. Most of the time, they would be discussing the nature of their next-door neighbour's business.

He was called Ali of Tehran and he sold exotic rugs from Hamadan and Shiraz, which was very much okay. Nobody had ever seen him selling any of his rather expensive rugs. So there was no way that he had the chance to make more money than the others in that street. He also sold water pipes, which he called 'hukkah', and one could sit in his rug shop to smoke shisa and hashish mixed with plain sweet tobacco.

He would also keep dhoop cubes of various sorts of scent in his shop, which were bought by Hindus for keeping their places of worship holy, for their uncountable Gods. The thing is both Hindus and Muslims have their own sort of incense to use for their own worshipping ceremonies to avoid confusion about their religious identity. Even the incense had to follow the rules of communalism among these two large communities. Who could have been offended, if such irregularities might take place, is not known though.

And that cute Bangladeshi middle-aged guy, selling green fresh lemon and ginger, and also sweetly scented, number one basmati rice coming from Pakistan. A Darjeeling tea with thick milk and sugar in a plastic cup was free, with one piece of his vegan *samocha*. His simple and roundish, broad smiling face had been often mistaken for a Pakistani face but such thoughtless remarks would dig bleeding wounds into his heart.

But he knew how to keep his upsets to himself by recalling the name of the mighty ten-handed goddess Durga: 'Ram, Ram. Krishna, Krishna.

God forbid, no, I am a Bangladeshi, who fought in the freedom fight as a child, against the Pakis in 1971. Thanks to all our Gods that finally we won that war. Long live the 16th of December 1971.' He would utter the date with pride and fright.

And there and then, he would turn and make a prayer to a small and dark clay statue of a deity, which was standing on a white wooden altar fixed on the wall, by bringing his two palms together just in front of his forehead, with the two hands as it were forming a lotus. The very mention of the name of that God-forbidden country Pakistan would wipe the smile off his face. He would fold both his palms together like in a prayer to greet people by saying 'Joy Bangla!'. What a calm and decent face he had!

And there was that exotic looking Turkish guy from Istanbul, who had a shop full of ladies' dresses decorated with tiny pieces of glass and fake pearls. The best thing he had were those large gilded mirrors of different sizes. One could also buy brass Aladdin's lamps from him. You name it and it was all to be found. Yeah! That was Achmed Gadir. What a polite and smiling face he had! A deep sigh again comes through her nostrils, causing the air to feel sad. 'Those good old days!' And those good old neighbours.

'The film is not done and the show must go on!'

2

Ab Ovo

In slow motion, they had all disappeared. Instead, loads of cheap coffee shops popped up overnight, like mushrooms in a fertile field in Poland or poppies growing in an Afghan valley. Those cafés are open till the early morning and by then the air outside is filled with a poignant odour. Not of coffee, but of hash and other smoke. It is all allowed in this city. The tourists who claim to be here to visit the Van Gogh museum or other museums, even the museum of Anne Frank, have taken a chair to rest here, in those basements, to have a dark cup of coffee. The other offers would come afterwards, incidentally.

This is the exotic city of Amsterdam, where one can have anything one wants. Tourists of all sorts come here to have the time of their lives. They can enjoy the basement life without any hesitation or feelings of guilt. You are here to enjoy your money and you don't need to be bothered by the outside world. They come and they go, leaving no marks behind.

This city has got this anonymous character. No one wants to know anyone. The doctors do not want to know their patients outside their practice. The physiotherapist would be terribly upset seeing the person who has come off the treatment bench just an hour before and who is now shopping for his or her ready-made evening meal in the same food hall, in the unmissable Albert Heijn supermarket. They try to avert their faces as much as possible and will do their best to remain unrecognised. Their privacy must remain inviolable in this untouchable vibrant city.

She looks around her. The sun has gone down quite a bit now. Its tired rays have reflected on the canal's pitch-dark filthy water. It is so thick with dirt that even a strong summer ray would not be able to penetrate it to change its colours. The whole town is full of canals like this one and the city is so proud of them. There are eighty-eight of them spread throughout the city. Tourists see them by taking a canal cruise. They can have lunch with herring sandwiches or even a candle-lit dinner on a glass-covered boat, floating through the canals.

A foreigner will always be encouraged to utter the phrase, *achtentachtig prachtige grachten*, producing the Dutch 'g' sound. Some of them will genuinely try to pronounce the unpronounceable words and some will laugh an unpleasant laugh. It is all so much fun! This city has so much to offer to tourists and to its own people. That's why they all want to come here and all want to stay here too. But eventually they leave, when their pockets are empty.

'Lucky me!' She produces a loud sigh. She had a lucky escape, not having to learn this difficult-sounding language. On the other hand, it might not have been so bad to learn it. She wanted to learn it. If she had been able to continue her studies, then probably she would have been able to learn it. But, Ah! A deep sigh again. One should not ask too much from life. Her own mother tongue is difficult enough. It has so many consonants used in one single sentence. Not to mention the grammatical complications. But she does not care much about languages anyway. She does not need any language in her job.

Where she grew up, in a tiny little village in Poland, a place close to the border of a very rich and powerful West European country, people are still struggling to emerge from the hardships of the Second World War, where their only luxury is to share their human body warmth during the hard, frosty winter. Not to mention the dogs and the cats. The household animals are more than welcome too to share the body heat. In extreme winters, every bit of heat is welcome.

She is now shivering with the thought of a distant cold from a distant past. Cold or no cold, she will go back there. Of course she will, when the time is ripe. She will certainly return, when all the demands are fulfilled. She will clean the air. She will bring fresh oxygen, enough for every filthy heart. She will be the legend they wanted her to be!

Her thoughts make her look around her again. A bulky looking guy is peeping through the windows into the basement room where she works. The red curtains are half drawn. The bright red light is burning outside the window. Only, no window-doll in a short crimson dress is visible.

She looks at the guy. He is clean shaven today and wearing a pair of old Wrangler jeans and a black T-shirt. She studies him again. He does not look much better than he normally does, she thinks. In fact, his unshaven, woolly look fits him better. And the black T-shirt? Probably he has bought it for one and a half euros from the Albert Cuyp market. And those old, shabby shoes. Eek! Shoes?

He does not recognise her. He does not even look at her properly. He is still looking at her window, probably hoping to see her gleaming body. She looks at him and feels a kind of pity for this lonely middle-class guy. She does not feel like getting up, going inside and changing her outfit. She glances at her dark green rubber boots which look almost black.

Inside these boots, her feet are wrapped up in a pair of thick purple woollen socks. She has always had those socks on. She has cold feet throughout the year. Those cold, wet feet! No, she does not want to feel that cold again, even though her rubber boots make her feet rather sweaty. Still, she always has the feeling that her feet are wet from the dirty water of the canal. These rubber boots give her a sense of cleanliness.

She likes to be clean. If she could, she would have a very clean bedroom of her own and a very clean bed. She would change the bed sheets every day and put white cotton sheets on her bed, preferably Egyptian cotton. And she would have a bath. Nothing fancy, but a simple, white little bath in the corner of her small room.

She would buy some nice smelling bathing salts to put in the warm water and sit in the bath during the winter evenings, when the winter wind would be blowing hard outside, shaking the thin, old glass windows of her room and she would be enjoying her bath, sitting in the scented water, holding a beautiful book of classical Persian poetry in her hands, like those princesses in the Arabian tales, and being very careful not to drop the book of poems into the nice clean water.

And there will be someone, someone she has never met, suddenly coming in, uninvited, bringing her a mug of scented herbal tea and smiling at her, handing her a white cotton towel fresh from the laundry, inviting her into the dream of a clean, spotless world!

She looks at her rubber boots now. They are dirty and certainly not white. From the moment she started working there, she had made it clear to Visigoth that he must let her work in her rubber boots. And Visigoth was not bothered about her demands. Who cares about a pair of rubber boots anyway? People who come here don't care much about such trifles.

They come for the real thing and they want the real thing to be done very quickly. They are in a hurry. They have got families and kids to take care of. This city keeps its time for every little detail. Sins or good deeds, rights or wrongs, all are marked and pointed out.

But her hair was a different matter. Visigoth had a drawn-out and terrifying argument with her about her long and shiny high blond hair. The hair that her mother liked so much. Her mother, who would comb her long shiny hair with an ancient wooden comb and make two thick braids, which would be hanging from her neck towards her chest. A dark champagne-coloured ribbon would be hanging from the ends of those two braids. How proud they both were of those two braids, not only the fact that she had such lovely blond hair, but also that her hair was combed with such a very rare comb! What an extraordinary comb that was!

Her mother told her that that comb had come from Granada, a historical place in Spain, that it was an ancient comb from a noble lady of her ancestral family, who was a famous queen of her time and from whom she was a direct descendant. Who knows? Maybe she has one or two royal genes. But nowadays, she has her doubts. That is simply because Granada in Spain is very far from her tiny little village, which shares its borders with a very rich and powerful country.

But Visigoth had a point too. It is all about his customers. What they want, Visigoth must produce. He is not going to lose his clients to a next-door rival. Business is business and no one is a friend in the world of business. The tall, white, middle-aged and middle-class unattractive guys want petite Asian-looking girls, preferably with dark hair. *Belle Klein*, small beauty. Like the iron statue of that small, robust beauty standing in an iron frame, in front of the church, declaring and demanding the rights of workers in civilization's oldest profession.

She feels lucky that she is not so tall. In fact she is no taller than the average Asian girl – although she cannot really call herself 'a girl' any more. All those years of studying in the Medical faculty have taken a good part of her lifetime. The internship and then working as a doctor here and there, that all cost a lot of her precious time. But even then, there still remains a girl-like look on her face.

Visigoth did not look at her body. But her hair. It was very, very off-putting. Blond was out. Even the Arabs did not appreciate blondes anymore. Suddenly they all wanted a small, brownish girl with darkish hair. Dark goes very well with purple-red outfits, the so-called *harkini*, a miniscule version of a bikini, the shortest dress that has ever existed for the work of a harlot.

The lower part of the harkini is a triangular piece of velvety material, a mini-version of a 'tanga' and the top part is a sort of hard-wired push-up bra. It pushes the bust so high up that the breasts almost touch the chin. This only makes her uncomfortable and she has her doubts about those push-up bras. She has never noticed that any of her clients got aroused due to that ingenious piece of garment.

The families who are living in the apartments above her basement working place often see her sitting behind the glass window in that 'harkini' and she really has not noticed any reaction from them. No matter what sex they are, they have never shown any interest in her boobs, except for the babies of course.

The sucklings gaze intensely at her two small and brownish bare nipples, which are resting on the top of her wired harkini, while their saliva is running like old syrup coming out of a bottle that is being poured on top of a farmhouse pancake. But at least these cute and always hungry babies are honest about their feelings. To put it bluntly, she has never thought that her rather sagging breasts had any power to attract attention from either sex, simply because they have never been an item of beauty.

But nothing was a big deal. The next-door Chinese neighbour has advice on everything. Huh! Those good old Chinese ladies with their knowledge of power. Their sun-bench had made her pale-white skin brownish and a long wig of real shiny black hair had transformed her from a small Polish world to a large street market in Bangkok in no time. She had looked in the big mirror standing in the corner of the nail-and-hair shop. In Dutch, with a very high-pitched Chinese voice, the Chinese nail lady had asked her, smiling, 'Who are you now?'

She looked at her own image in the large mirror and not recognising herself, she said, 'Who is that?' The Chinese nail-and-hair lady had smiled a large, proud smile. 'You see, I am a facialist, an expert on faces. Worked very hard in Hong Kong's porn industry. An artist of the world! Those were the days, when I had everything. Well, almost everything.' She let go a deep sigh and in an indifferent tone asked the Chinese artist, 'Well then, what are you doing here?' The Chinese artist looked taken aback and also in an indifferent tone said, 'Ach! Not old age, mind you. I have been there! I have seen it all.'

She smiled at the Chinese facialist and make-up artist lady with huge gratitude. These good old knowledgeable Chinese ladies, who are full of experience of all kinds. They are everywhere and they are always there when you need them for whatever reason. She mumbled a 'thank you' to her with genuine gratitude. The facialist lady suddenly looked melancholy and, smiling a sad smile to her, asked, 'What is your name, my dear? You see, names are very important in this business.' She was searching for a name for herself. A good name for this job.

Well, her own name had been good enough for everything so far. Her name, given to her when she was born, had been always good for her. 'Posette. My name is Posette.'

The Chinese facialist in the nail-and-hair shop looked horrified, as if she wanted to scream. Posette did not understand why. Her name had been good for her childhood, for her village church, for her school, for her eccentric piano teacher. Even for the medical faculty and even as a doctor! None of her patients had said that her name did not fit with her job.

Posette looked puzzled. 'Well, my name is actually Charlemagne. I am a descendant of an old royal house from Granada, in Spain.' The Chinese lady smiled with relief and joyfully she said, 'Oh, Cher! Your name is Cher! That is a very suitable name for this perfect job!'

She did not care much for her new name. She came back to the basement where Visigoth had been waiting for her. She was deep in thought. 'Will Visigoth be able to recognise me? How shall I introduce myself to him? Shall I tell him my new name immediately?' But nothing was necessary. In this job, a name did not require as much attention

as she had been told by the Chinese facialist artist.
A name was needed only for the unwritten records.

Visigoth did not look at her for long and indicated
with a gesture that someone was waiting and she
should go in. In a low, deep voice he warned her,
'Don't you dare to scream.' She looked up at him
and shivered. His bloodless, dreadful, cold white
face showed immense hatred and there was no
mercy in his hollow dead eyes.

And that was it. She entered the basement room.
She knew instinctively that the red curtain had to
be drawn. As soon as the curtain was closed, a
bright red light started burning on the street side
of the window and the glow of that light lit up the
room inside in a crimson red, as if a horrifying
red colour had smeared the whole of the universe.
That crimson red, she was not really prepared for.
That must be the colour of a non-refundable sale!

'The film is not done and the show must go on!'

3

The Nativity

A shadow falls on her body from the back and a familiar unpleasant smell hits her nostrils. A smile lights up her gloomy face. This stink makes her happy, as if she has been waiting for something like this to wake her up and bring her back to her working street. Eek! The horrible stink must be coming from his leather jacket.

That old brown oversized sheepskin jacket, hanging to his knees, which is probably the only outdoor clothes he has. Whenever he has to say something about this jacket, he mentions his grandfather, about whom most of them doubt whether he really is his grandfather or not. The jacket originally belonged to this grandfather, the Chief, who lives high up in the Arizona Mountains.

The ancient Chief, who had never come down

to the plains, even for a cup of coffee, hating the thought that he might have to shake hands with a white guy whose ancestors had murdered the rest of his clan. That had happened many years ago and their history had changed in manifold ways since then. Yet the clan needed a new heir for themselves.

This was not because the old Chief had been growing old every day. Not at all. That would be out of the question. The ageless Chief was still able to do loads of things that the young ones would hardly dare to do. He had shared his life with many loving and lovely souls and, even today, he was not without love. The fire never went out in his tent and there were young ones ready to make him happy and, in return, make themselves proud.

But all that fun had remained fruitless. Once there was one, who had given the Chief an heir. That one, a lovely brown but almost white lady, had somehow been crossing the Arizona Mountains with a group of gypsies and the Chief could not close his eyes for many days, till one evening she came into the Chief's tent to perform an evening prayer with the clan.

They had been looking to the moon together, witnessing the stars dancing in pairs in the fields of the Milky Way, while the others were watching them, standing together, holding each other's hands. The whole clan had witnessed their togetherness that night. It was going to be the most festive night that the clan had ever celebrated.

The Chief finally had an heir. When the cry of the new-born babe was heard, the female folks of the higher ranks entered into the tent of the new mother and took the baby, wrapped in sheepskin, to show it to the important members of the clan. They remained stern and calm, waiting for a sign from the Chief. The Chief looked at the baby and closed his eyes.

The important ones looked up at the sky for an answer and also closed their eyes. It felt as if the air on the Arizona Mountains was drained of oxygen and the whole clan seemed stupefied, not knowing whether to shout in joy or shut their mouths in despair.

In their bewilderment, an unthinkable possibility had arisen: what if the baby was a female child? In the ocean-dead silence, they all tried to read each other's minds, but after a while their faces broadened with a thin smile, which said to each other, 'No, that cannot be'. That had never happened throughout the history of this ancient clan. Someone like the Chief was born to crown the clan with certain things like a male heir. In fact, many heirs, and that process had never gone wrong, so far.

That baby was certainly the male heir for the clan, who would shine like a gold star over their Arizona Mountains. They were all absolutely certain that there could be no mistake about this, as they had been taught to have faith in their own 'Nature' around them.

In the meantime, the hungry baby started to cry and one of the ladies brought the baby into the tent of its mother. But the tent was empty. The mother of the new-born had disappeared, just like that. And no one ever bothered with the simple question: where could that whitish gypsy woman have gone in this severe cold, having just delivered a whitish baby to the earth?

In the meantime, the whitish baby was becoming more and more white every day and when he came of age, he wanted to know who he was. The boundless shame of his question lingered around like the stink of dead enemies in days gone by.

The whole clan was consumed by shame, as he

even denied the mother who had fed him. That was a horrible betrayal of the honour of mother's milk. How could he ever be a Chief in the future? How would he ever be able to take care of his people? How did he dare to insult his own father, the oldest Chief of the Arizona Mountains?

They all felt a secret pity for him, with a shameful deep sigh. They all agreed that, after all, there had to be some white blood cells inside one of the four chambers of his heart. By denying the milk-mother, he had denied the honour of all the mothers in the Universe of the Arizonian Indian clans, which was not that small an area, if one thought about it.

But white or brown, the Chief's heir did not behave like the other members of his clan. In fact, he started behaving more and more like a crazy white guy, the kind of person the clan knew about only from ancient stories told by their ancestors. Often he would go down to the white town and buy a pair of tight jeans and some coffee.

Oh yes, how he liked drinking coffee day and night. He had no respect for the rules and customs of his clan and hardly any for his father, the Chief. Many rare beauties had tried to win his heart. But all their efforts and effrontery were in vain. He kept his heart to himself.

One day, he came to the top of the mountain, walking like a tired bear and went directly into the Chief's tent, where his father was being taken care of by some rare beauties. He did not even bow to his father the Chief. The ladies covered their elegant noses with their hands; even the Chief was annoyed that the boy had learned from the white folks the disgusting habit of smoking grass, what they called hashish. Why didn't he have a homemade smoke, which would knock him out for a couple of weeks at least? And that hot-headed behaviour of white men? Simply disgusting. But the heir did not care much. He looked directly into the Chief's eyes and asked, 'Where is my mother? How did you make her disappear?'

For the very first time probably the Chief got annoyed with his heir. His eyes glanced down and his hands went up in the form of a prayer. An elderly woman in buffalo-skin clothes slowly entered into the tent and made a curtsey to the Chief. In a very thin low voice she said, 'Listen to me, you, the one. I am your milk-mother. Nobody made nobody disappear. Your birth mother was just gone. She just did not want to take you with her. Don't you see, you were a white baby! And she was a brownish Gypsy lady.'

'I don't care a bit for your story,' the heir roared. 'Look, my milk-mother; I thank you for saving me by suckling. But I need my real mother. Now where is she? Where did she come from?'

'I don't know. I am sorry, my dear one.'

Tears rolled down her pale cheeks.

'I thought that I would be as good as your own mother. I had high hopes that one day you would take care of me, when I would be old and frail. You did not even care to know about my misfortunes. After giving you my milk, no-one would have my milk anymore, not because I suckled you but because I did not want to feed any of the others.'

Shame was breaking her into pieces.

In a despondent voice she continued, 'Imagine all my stillborn sons, who were not around to demand their mother's milk. They too wanted to give their share of milk to someone else like you! Someone whose mother was not there to hold them in their motherly arms! And now, look at you and see how you have even hurt the souls of my stillborn loving ones, who are still around, watching me from above!'

But he did not have the heart to understand his milk-mother's plea. He was pushing the cow skin rug on the floor of the tent vehemently as if a bull was fighting with its hooves. His whole attitude was afire. Finally the Chief had to give up his Chiefly grace. He looked up at him with a knife-sharp glare and in a deep voice said, 'Your biological mother was a Gypsy lady. If she is alive, she must have joined her caravan, going somewhere in the plains.'

The heir listened and asked, 'Okay then, where did the Gypsies come from?' Now the Chief said nothing. His eyes closed again. Another, younger lady whispered, 'Your mother was not just like the other Gypsies. You must know that she was born somewhere in a place called Nepal or something like that! She was an adventurer. She wanted to see the white world. She is not like one of us!'

Not taking any notice of her, he asked in a maddened voice, 'And where is that place called Nepal?' In a meek and frightened voice, she whispered, 'I am not sure. Maybe it is at the foot of the Mountains, below, where white men move.' She started to shiver violently, whether because it was freezing cold outside or whether out of fear of the presence of the Chief, no-one knew.

And so, the Chief's heir left the tent and went down the mountain, to trail his Gypsy mother, who was in fact a whitish brown lady, who had given birth prematurely to a white baby, while enjoying the status of a queen with the Indian Chief of the Arizona Mountains. But the need for a new leader remained in the clan, like a large empty bombshell. An heir they needed. And why not? They thought about the world below them, the world of the white men.

Everyone needs a leader, whether one is an Arizonian Indian or not. One even needs a leader for UKIP in the UK, or someone like Trump in the USA. The leader can even be a xenophobic Dutch politician, an extreme populist, full of hatred against humankind, whose own dark hair is painted high blond only so that he will be accepted as a white person. But how can he hide his own face, which resembles his Indonesian grandmother? He hates foreigners with dark hair, especially those who are noticeably Muslims. Funny that no one has ever bothered to ask him, 'How much does it cost to be blond? Or are you ashamed of your Asian connection? Do you enjoy being a populist crow, covering your body with peacock feathers?'

And how about that Orchid lady of Burma or Myanmar? Was she awarded a Nobel prize, only to finish the unfinished job of a warmonger sadist Buddhist monk, who had started to demolish the Rohinga Muslims by using the method of ethnic cleansing? And how about those world famous leaders who have received many prizes and superlative adjectives, who have removed the word 'peace' from every corner of the Middle East?

The Chief of Arizona's need was not so dire as that of those cheap politicians.

Leaders like the Chief had never thrown out the elected government of any country by force, only to loot their oil and ancient treasures! The Chief had no hatred and no greed in his clean heart, which was full with the fresh oxygen of the clean air of the top of the Arizonian Mountains. He knew the value of his own clan, who were all clean-hearted souls, belonging to the Old Man above.

That was the beginning of the story of the Arizona Chief's grandson in Amsterdam, who had been appointed as the next Chief of the clan. The old Chief had offered him his only sheepskin jacket, as a token of his new status as the future 'Chief'. The jacket was decorated with multi-coloured beads and feathers of hawks sewn into it. And since then, he had worn it faithfully. But that was all such a long story too.

By pure chance, he had been there, in the Mountains of Arizona, and by some miracle, he had met the Chief of Arizona. The almost ancient Chief had started chanting a ritual, acknowledging his familiar smell and they all took him as the Chief's grandson. No one had any doubt about his identity and no one asked him to prove anything according to the rituals of the clan, like cutting the palm of his right hand while holding the knife in his left hand. No such ancient rituals were required.

The clan were very modern nowadays. The Chief's advisory board went down to the white-men's town to find a hospital where they could check the DNA of the Chief's grandson, the new heir. The doctor was told the reason, how bad it would be if the Chief of the Mountains were not to leave a true bloodline of his origin behind.

But the clan did not need to worry. The grandson had the same DNA as the Chief. No-one had any doubt that the grandson was indeed the son of the

Chief's white heir, who had gone to search for his own mother and had never been heard of again ever since.

The only sad thing was that this grandson of the Chief also did not know where his mother was. He had also been searching for his own mother. And one fine very early misty morning, before the sun had risen to show the right paths to the souls of the Arizona Mountains by its pure morning light, the Chief's grandson had also left the fire of the warm tent at the top of the Arizonian Mountains, not waking up even the most faithful dog!

'The film is not done and the show must go on!'

4

Depayse

Okay. That's a fine story. But the stink! Sometimes that nose-hurting stink is unbearable. 'He needs a bath,' she thinks. Or perhaps he can take a long shower in her workplace, when nobody is watching. Sometimes, some very careful clients take a long shower without soap, so that they will not smell of sin when they return to their homes. And no one must smell any fragrance of any cosmetics. One has to be so careful these days. One does not want to get caught out by any careless act. Hypothetically speaking, why must anyone suspect the obvious?

The long arm of the shadow pulls down his ancient hat, covering half of his face and a different sort of pungent air hits her nostrils. She knows that there is a greasy dark brown hat on his head, which has a bullet hole going through it, and throughout the years, the hole has been getting bigger and bigger. Rumour has it that the hat might have belonged to his long lost father, the person he has probably never met. But those are not his own words. Anyway, that hat is also a part of his habits, inseparable from his jacket.

She smiles an affectionate smile and says, 'You are blocking my sun, Chief.' He returns a gloomy laugh.

'It is time to work, Pos. A guest is hanging around by the window.'

Posette's face changes in a second.

'Don't call me Pos anymore, Chief.'

'Why not? You are the most positive person I have ever known. It will be okay one day, dear positive girl.'

There is a knife-cutting sharp feeling inside her head. Someone has got hold of her hair at the back, while the melancholic words of the Chief are still ringing in her ears. But there is a different tall shadow now covering her whole body. The unexpected shadow of a misogynist. She screams, 'Let go! You are hurting me. Let my hair go!' But he does not let her hair go. He pulls her up by her hair and in a rough, deep voice growls at her, 'Now, you dirty little slut, don't you know who I am?'

'Yes! Yes I do.'

She mumbles again, 'Please let me go, please!'

He is shaking her head by pulling her hair.

'Okay, little whore, who am I?'

'You are – you are Visigoth,' she says, shivering.

'Well, Visigoth who? Tell me all about myself.'

His strong biceps are covered with the tattoos of Malaysian pythons. And the pythons are trying to suffocate her. She feels the need for air in her lungs. Gasping, she says, 'You are Visigoth Wamba, an Afrikaner from South Africa, from Johannesburg. You are an absconded police officer. You were in trouble there and you had to run away and if they ever catch you – if, only.'

'Enough,' and he slaps her hard on her cheek. She does not have any tears. Her head is bent down; she feels abashed. If only the Chief did not have to witness this abuse. If only he were not here, at this horrifying moment.

'Stop humiliating her, Visigoth. You can't insult her like that on the streets.'

She smiles now. Yes, that is him. That is the Chief of Amsterdam!

The tall and thin South African turns to the

Chief with huge disdain.

'And why not, may I ask? She is a little whore and she is my whore. The clients are waiting for her and she is having a chat with you on my steps? Remember? The steps that you have not paid for the last couple of months?'

The Chief feels extremely irritated by his remarks.

'Look, friend, me not paying the rent has got nothing to do with insulting a lady in such a brutal manner.'

There is irony in Visigoth's voice as he mocks the Chief and says, 'Oh, that sounds pretty holy, doesn't it?'

'Visigoth, listen to me. That lady is a doctor. She is not like the others,' the Chief says in a calm voice. Now Visigoth turns to him and growls, 'Eh, and why are you so much bothered by it? Does she resemble your own mother? Hey, does she?'

His words are not even finished when an enormous blow lands on his nose. Visigoth falls to the street, calling on his own mother, swearing in Afrikaans in a form that does not have any resemblance with Dutch or any other language at this moment.

Posette claps her hands like a little child that is enjoying herself and shouts, 'Hey, Chief, I did not know that your hands were so strong. Look how his nose is bleeding. Ha ha. Ha ha good, very good.'

All of a sudden, she starts saying something in an unintelligible language, very fast. A shadow of fear has taken away her childish joy in a second and her face turns pale like blotting paper. There is a police car moving towards them in slow motion. Visigoth sees them coming too. He can't afford any trouble in his business and the other partners are not going to be amused either.

Visigoth stands up and wipes his nose. He pulls up his very short T-shirt and hisses like a snake, 'I'll see you, Chief. I'll send you to Arizona, to that shit of your grandfather.'

Then he turns to Posette. His iron fist, with its extremely large fingers, is about to come up but suddenly he steps back as if struck by lightning. His eyes are full of fear. He is transformed into a frozen person in a fraction of a moment.

Posette is puzzled and follows his gaze. The police car has stopped at the cul-de-sac and a specially designed wheelchair is moving towards them. Posette also feels fear creeping up on her.

It freezes her as if she has seen a serpent next to her feet. The wheelchair is coming towards them. A medium-sized, well-built young guy is pushing it from the back. The guy is wearing shiny black leather clothes and has silver jewellery all over him, except for his gold earrings.

But the burly lady in the wheelchair looks very majestic in her outfit. It is still rather warm outside in this autumn afternoon but her large body is covered in a very expensive black mink coat. On her head is a decorative African head cover. A large diamond and emerald brooch is hanging from the top of her forehead, just like one of those Indian Maharajas. If one had not known who she was, one might have thought of her as a queen of somewhere.

'Lucretia,' she whispers. 'Chief, it is Lucretia. I am done for. Today, I am caught red-handed. Oh, Chief, where am I to go?'

The Chief has been watching the wheelchair too.

'The wheelchair – the wheel of fortune!'

The Chief is whispering too. But he has to say something to calm her down. He has to support her to overcome her fear.

Posette comes to stand next to him and she

holds his hands. In a child-like voice, she says, 'Hey Chief, I did not know your thin fingers were so strong. But what now? Madam is going to throw me out of this street.'

There is agitation in her voice and tears start rolling down her cheeks. The Chief takes her silky fingers in his hand, gives them a soft push and says, 'Have faith. It is still a beautiful world.'

The wheels of the expensive wheelchair have stopped in front of them. Without looking at the guy behind her, the lady says in a harsh tone, 'And what are you looking at? Never forget that you are gay.'

From behind her the frightened guy says in a meek voice, 'Well, I thought she is beautiful.'

'Well, she was beautiful. But not now, Visigoth has thrown her out. She would not be good enough now even for the streets near the Central Station.'

The madam looks at her and asks, 'You are Char, aren't you?'

'What now?' She tries to open her mouth to correct the lady about her name but the lady has in the meantime raised her small left hand, rings with huge pieces of diamond, emerald and ruby shining from all five fingers, signalling that it does not matter whether one is called 'Char' or 'Cher' on these streets. Because every Cher's life is completely charred anyway. Then she looks at the Chief and says, 'You know, Chief, the men of your tribe have always protected their women. Their mothers and sisters and wives never had anything to fear. Take her home.'

'Home! I haven't got a home?'

While the Chief is saying this, Posette takes his hand with both her hands, holding it tight as if she is frightened to lose her priceless toy. The madam's lips tremble, which perhaps looks like a smile, and she says, 'Yes, you have a home.'

The Chief makes a hopeless gesture, shaking his head, and says, 'Madam, I live on the top floor of this house, where there is no bed, no toilet and only a little wash-basin. I am lucky there is cold running water. There is one light bulb, without a shade. I sleep on a sofa-bed that I have collected from the street. I have not paid the rent for a couple of months. Soon I'll also be on the street. Visigoth is not going to spare me. How can I take care of this lady?'

The madam looks at him for a long time and says in a soothing voice, 'Of course you can take care of her. You are the grandson of the Chief of Arizona, aren't you? Didn't he check your DNA when you went to meet him last time in the mountains? Didn't you see how the great Chief takes care of his clan?'

'But, but that is a very different situation. And I, I–' He doesn't know enough words to answer her.

'I am Lucretia, who was found under the stone bench of 'Jardin du Soraya' in Granada as a new-born babe and brought up by the great Gypsy clan. I was the most famous flamenco dancer of Spain. Before coming to this place, I toured the whole Western world and the South of Asia and won the hearts of many.'

He looks agitated as if he wants to say, 'So what?' But he doesn't have the chance to reply, as she continues.

'Money came along with the broken hearts. I had chests of drawers full of broken hearts as well as banknotes and diamonds. Look around, Chief. Both sides of the canals belong to me. I am the owner of the houses which are standing alongside the canals. When I bought them, they said I was crazy. They said I was throwing my money away in the dirty waters of those canals.'

'There was no-one to rent those houses to at that time. Every tenant had a right to live in a rented house the first three weeks for free. And I did not charge them anything. The poor girls took shelter here and we made money from shiny men with scented banknotes in their coat pockets! And look at them now. They are renting my properties and insects like Visigoth are keeping my drawers full.'

She makes a gesture and her wheelchair starts to move backwards. Probably, she does not feel like enjoying her canal tour anymore.

They watch her move away. Lucretia, the most famous Spanish flamenco dancer and the notorious harlot of Amsterdam, who is now as ancient as the history of this place. Who moves like the queen of ancient Granada. Is it possible that Lucretia is in some bizarre way connected to her? Or to all of them?'

The rays of the sun have almost drowned in the dark canal waters. They go up the steep staircase to the top floor. The staircase is so narrow that one can hardly go up walking straight. One has to bend one's legs in a strange kind of way to reach the top floor. Right after opening the door, she is confronted by a large poster picture of an old

American Indian, which is hanging on the wall from a rusty nail.

The Indian on the poster has a large, brown, complicated face and his cunning eyes are as sharp as an eagle. His long hair is woven in two thick braids, which are hanging across his chest. The Indian is gazing intensely as if he wants to see through her heart. She says, 'Don't you look at me so critically! I also used to have such braids, you know? And don't you try to scare me. I mean no harm to anyone and you know that, don't you?'

The old wooden floor is bare. Only a shabby sofa-bed is standing in a corner. On the bare windowsill is a little black and white photograph of a young girl, thirteen or fourteen years of age, in a non-western dress, in a brown wooden frame. The photograph has faded so much that the girl's face is no longer clearly visible. The wooden frame is old and shabby. But compared with the rest of the room, the picture is well dusted and kept clean, as if the little photograph is a kind of altar and does not belong here.

There is a little square skylight between the wooden beams of the roof. The last bit of daylight is falling through it. There is a broken electric kettle standing under the little wash-basin, a couple of used paper cups and a tiny towel hanging from a dirty broken nail from the wall. The towel is so dirty that it is not possible to recognize its original colour. One or two pieces of underwear and a T-shirt are hanging from the side of the sofa-bed. And an unwashed synthetic single blanket is pushed away under the sofa.

Suddenly she misses her sleeping place in the corner of those red rooms. After all, those were clean in a literal sense. There were bed sheets and towels, washed at 90 degree Centigrade, spin-dried and ironed. And there was always scented soap. If only people like Visigoth were a bit more human. But on the other hand, she had not been allowed to sleep on those money-making fancy water-beds. Those beds had no blankets or pillows. Instead, she slept inside the large closet of the boudoir, where she could wrap herself in clean sheets.

Her deep thoughts about all this are broken by the Chief.

'Why did not you go with that client?'

It is as if the Chief can read her mind.

'I mean this place is nothing for you. And I have nothing.'

His eyes are becoming steamy red and, for the first time in his life, he feels like a complete nothing. All of a sudden, he wants to have so much.

He would like to have so many things to entertain this lady, who has been his neighbour for several years and who actually is a harlot. But no! No. He corrects himself. She is a doctor, who has taken care of many patients in her native village, somewhere in Poland, for free. She has already done so many good deeds in her life! One day he'll declare her a saint. Only if–. He can't think anymore.

Posette looks up at the sky.

'You see, Chief, that guy is an addict. No. Not to a dangerous drug. But to his mobile phone. He likes to play games on his expensive iPhone and he cannot do that at home. His family does not even know that he has got a thing called iPhone! You see, Chief, half of the people are now addicted to mobile phones and they don't talk to each other anymore either!'

'And what's wrong with that?'

The Chief is looking at her questioningly, with a slight irritation. She does not answer him. There are certain things she cannot say to him. He keeps a distance from everything. All she can say is, 'Look, Chief, it is not easy to explain. He plays the games and I am just there watching him play. It is not really working. It is not like working and earning money. It is not honest, you see.'

The Chief nods knowingly. But she knows he does not understand what she means.

For she has not told him all of it. She could not tell him the shameful part of it. She could not tell him that while the old guy was playing games on his mobile phone, she also had to play games with certain parts of his body in a certain way. How often she would vomit and how often Visigoth was there to make her eat her own dirt. The humiliation that she had to endure each moment of her life as a harlot!

How often she has wanted to disappear. In her most vivid nightmares, how she has enjoyed the scene of seeing her own dead body floating in the waters of the dirty canal. But she had no choice. She did not dare to run. She was frozen with fear. Not that Visigoth would remove her to an unknown place in Johannesburg, but there was something else. The fear of losing her own face. The fear of not keeping her commitments and failing them.

Yes, she has run away many times in her life and that brought her nothing. Now she has to do things. She must help others. Others who have nothing, And now, she has the opportunity to make a choice. She is finally free to make a choice. She is under a roof which belongs to a lady called Lucretia of Jardin du Soraya. And a strange guy is with her, who has nothing but himself. Yes, she is not alone. She has nothing to fear. Because the Chief is with her. Yes, the Chief is here.

'The film is not done and the show must go on!'

5

Del Gratia

The very last bit of light has faded from the sky. The city is not lit up enough to light the top part of the room. A helicopter is moving over the houses with a horrible noise. Posette looks outside through the window and asks, 'Who are those guys in the helicopter? And why are they flying over these houses?'

He shakes his head in an indifferent gesture and says, 'Probably they are from the narcotics department of the police. They are looking for houses that might have plants growing inside.'

'What do you mean? What plants?'

She sounds rather silly, he thinks. How is it possible that she does not know about these practices in this city?

He wants to remain silent but says, 'Plants that

are not exotic vegetables from the East, but drugs. The space inside has to be very warm to grow them, so the houses are kept extremely hot for that reason. They can detect the over-heated houses from the sky.'

'Oh, really!? But I have never seen those guys before! And our basements are full of drugs! Why bother flying helicopters to detect the plant growers? How much grass can they grow in a tiny space of thirty square metres or so?'

He feels irritated now. Listlessly he says, 'Yes there are drugs in every corner of this country. Even in remote villages, where there is no shop where you can buy a loaf of healthy brown bread. But there are drugs to be bought on every side of every street. And why not? The government gets tax from the drugs money. In return, they have also set up many rehab centres.'

She knows that too. Drug addicts and pushers are getting free drugs and free syringes as a form of treatment by the government. There is also free alcohol for alcohol addicts. And their parents and families are getting free counselling. Psychologists and psychiatrists are over-worked. Social workers are working day and night. Nothing to complain about.

This is the sad reason that is destroying the lives of the have-nots while others are benefiting from the situation. For them, it is the reason they have good, well-paid jobs so they can afford to pay for their expensive mortgages as well as maddening mistresses. Not to mention, unaffordable private secretaries. But she must know all about these things! She has been connected with this sort of life for many years now. Is she really so naive? Or is she playing stupid, he wonders.

'Oh, yes, Chief, I know, I know. It is all so well arranged. Very smart of the Dutch government, don't you think? I have heard of it from someone. Someone who is well connected. You see, Chief, down in the basements, you see loads of things. But you don't know a lot of them.' She is searching for another topic of conversation now.

He too has got tired of this everyday talk. Drugs are not unknown and have not been kept a secret from the people of this country. Every household has a corner for drugs. Parents and children share their precious weekends together by also sharing drugs of all kinds. Life is bearable only if there is something in addition to life itself. People may not need food for their stomachs. But they certainly need something extra to mess up their brains. Otherwise life would simply not be tolerable.

Yeah, life and drugs, they are just like identical twins. One is meaningless without the other one. People want to be famous, so they can afford to have them aplenty. Other people are living in the gutter, because they have wasted all they had on this silken fun. How do they cope with their daily lives?

'I could be many things, Chief. But believe me, I don't do drugs. I hate that. That is something for horribly selfish people, who destroy their own lives as well as those around them,' she says intently.

The Chief says carelessly, 'There is one thing I know, which is, I'll never touch any drugs whatsoever, in my living life on this planet and I will never return to the mother earth, abusing loved ones because my head is not clear! I promised that to my mother!'

He just says it softly. She turns to him and with childish excitement says, 'Your mother, Chief? Where is she? Can I meet her?'

'No. You can't meet her.'

The answer sounds very cold and she wants to

argue with him. She wants to say, 'And why not? Is that because of what I do for a living?' But she does not dare to utter any word on this subject any more. She cannot see his face. But she feels a cold wind shaking her, making her feel frozen.

She feels the need for some warmth.

'Well then, Chief. Shall we say that you take the sofa and I take the bed?'

As soon as she has said it, she wants to correct her mistake and says, 'Well there is no bed, of course. Sorry. I know that. Well, I suppose there is only one blanket. Ha! Okay. We'll share it. I know how to share things. Don't you worry about me, Chief. I don't feel cold that much.'

He feels that she has started shivering. He pulls out his only blanket from under the sofa and an unpleasant smell fills the room. She wants to put her hands to her nose. But instead, she goes to open the window. As she tries to do so, a gust of wind hits the window and the little photograph falls to the floor, making a thin sound.

He shouts out loud, like a mad cry, 'Don't you never ever touch that photo. Never ever. Do you hear me?'

She wants to say that she did not mean to

touch it. That all she wanted to do was open the window, to let some fresh air into the room. But she says nothing. She feels overwhelmed. What a day she has been having! The police helicopters are moving over the house and a pale light is being reflected into the room. Her throat feels dry as if she is somewhere like the Sahara. She wants to drink some water.

She has seen the wash-basin and is now searching for it. At the same time, probably, he can read her mind. He says, 'Don't drink too much water now. There is no toilet here.' She stops moving and wants to say something like, 'What about you?' But before she can ask the question, he says, 'Guys go behind the trees next to the canals for small needs. But the police are there to catch such criminals and you would have to pay a fine in 'cash', on the spot.'

She can't see his face in the darkness. All she is thinking is, how on earth is a guy living in a place where there is no toilet!

As if he can read her mind, he says, 'You don't know the history of these houses. The top floors were built for the servants and they needed neither heat nor toilets. It is all a matter of adapting to the situation. Just close your eyes and there will be a morning again.'

His voice sounds rather indifferent and listless. Yeah, morning? What sort of glory is the morning going to bring to her?

She is literally on the streets. Streets that she has always been afraid of. Perhaps she has made a mistake. Actually she has made a huge mistake to confront Visigoth. Perhaps, it would be better for her to go back to him and ask for forgiveness. Beg him on her knees? Perhaps working for him a few weeks for free? Who knows, perhaps that churlish man will forgive her. She will make him realise how special she really is for his booming business.

She is indeed unique for several reasons. There are many customers who will ask for her. Especially that one, the one she calls the 'monkey' so fondly. How much he appreciates her calling him by that word and how much he longs for her to utter that word! His most favourite word in the English dictionary, for which he could climb Mount Everest. Or perhaps not. But there is something between the word 'monkey' and him.

Once he had confided to her that he had begged his wife to call him a 'monkey' just once. But she had vehemently refused and, uttering the name of her holy shrine, had threatened that next time such a situation should occur in her bed she would certainly call his mother. This was a severe threat, not only to himself but to all of his family members, who belonged to different tribes in different valleys across the whole region of Pak-Afghan territory.

Her tummy shakes with laughter when she recalls the next bit of the story. She recalls his embarrassed, sobbing face when he had confided to her that before he could beg his wife for forgiveness, his mother had called him from the top of a mountain in the Khyber Pass, where she was attending a 'bride-viewing' gathering with some other prominent ladies of her tribe, for a handsome boy of a troublesome tribe in the valley of Ghwarband, who was her next of kin.

It was a horrible mobile phone again. These walking and moving iPhones have removed the privacy from every bit of life. These phones follow everyone to the most private places of all on the planet. Who is spying on whom cannot be known anymore. It is obvious that all humans are living in clear and open danger, which is actually created by humans. It is not only about not having any privacy at all in life. There is an even scarier part.

As citizens of the world, we love to be connected with each other in every corner of this planet. But do we know who is collecting non-stop data on us and for what purposes? Whether it is iPhones or androids, they are spying on 'us', the common citizens and somewhere, someone is playing God on us, collecting our life stories for who knows what reasons. Why do we need so much information about us to be shared?

Why does his mother need an iPhone, on the top of the Khyber Pass? His mother knows their bedroom, which is in the attic. Whenever she comes to visit them in the Netherlands, which is not that often, not like his friends' parents, she occupies their bed, because that is the only decent double-bed in their house, on which a fashionable person can lie down and stretch their legs in a comfortable way. His mother often gets horribly painful cramps in both her legs, towards the end of almost every night and that's why she needs a large bed to roll and move, as may be required.

His tiny mother, who is barely five feet tall, loves comfort and has eagle-sharp eyesight, which works like the radar of NASA. Their bedroom scenario was already visible to her, on her phone screen. From the top of the Khyber Mountain, she could see their bedroom and also could sense their situation. Her eyelids were moving in a rude sort of way, as she said, 'Well, your wife still looks beautiful. But you? Eek, you are still a monkey! What has come out of my body! Couldn't they help you in those foreign hospitals? Couldn't they make a real man out of an ugly ape?'

Apparently, he had wanted to tell his mother that his wife used to be beautiful, like a photo model such as Jerry Hall, which was true once upon a time. But not now. Now her sizes had changed for the larger digits. But his wife moved faster to the iPhone and looking at it, she gave a curious smile to her mother-in-law and said, 'Jee hain, Ammijan (yes dear mother). Your son wants me to call him a little 'monkey' too!'

'You shameless little beast! Many times worse than your own giraffe of a father. You bring your stupid head here right now and I'll smash your stupid little monkey head on the topmost rock of this mountain and I will–'

All they heard was a smash and the connection was broken off. His mother must have thrown away the mobile phone or must have smashed it on the rocks, perhaps taking it for his own monkey head. When his wife turned back to him, he was already fast asleep in his new male tanga underwear, which he had bought from Visigoth's basement shop. He had his right-hand thumb in his mouth, which was producing an incredible amount of yellowish saliva and his face had a pretty smile like a monkey, as if a baby ape was sleeping with a piece of ripe banana in its hands.

She used to miss him, when his visits were not that frequent. His needs were unique. He did not dare to undress in front of her because of his extremely hairy body features. All he asked for was to lie down on top of her, putting his head between her breasts and listening to her heartbeat, while he would talk about his unsolved work problems. His patients, who were constantly lying and cheating. And she would give her views on those subjects. She could almost see those scoundrels with her mind's eye and she was so angry with them for being so unkind to him. She felt the need to protect him by saying one little word, 'Monkey!'

'Oh my God!'

She is thinking aloud now. How hard it will be for him, not being able to find her! Where will he go from now on?

And there are the others. Others, who did not come only to spend some time with her. They literally came to abuse her body, for which they paid bountifully to Visigoth. They came to carry out their abominable fantasies on her, or inside her body. Visigoth got paid loads of cash by those perverts, who only came to do things which they would not dare to ask for at home.

They were all decent-looking, highly educated men in shiny and expensive suits, whose angel faces are supporting their heads, which were full of dirt. A very famous one used to come only to urinate inside her and he did not allow her to move until he was done. There was a great actor, who wanted to have a pee on her face. And there were others with disgusting demands, which she fulfilled for money. These were all everyday matters and they will certainly ask for her. Visigoth will have no choice but to hire her again.

In the dark she is searching for an answer, when he says, 'Visigoth is a very inventive guy in the field of torture. I would not go near him again, if I were you. There are plenty of young girls on the streets and he awaits none.'

'But, Chief, I have left something there. Something very special to me,' she says in a sad voice. He says calmly, 'Nothing on Earth could be more special than your own life.'

'But it is. It really is. I have never let it go out of my hands in my whole life till now. You see, it is something that belongs to my mother!'

He turns to her in the dark and asks, 'From your mother? What is that thing?'

He seems agitated again.

'The comb. The wooden comb! My mother's ancestral comb from Granada, Spain. My mother gave it to me. Oh, Chief, I have never been without it since I was born.'

Now her sobs turn into a desperate cry.

He is silent for a while and then says, 'We have to wait till tomorrow morning. Then Berenguela will be there. She will find a way for you.'

'Who is Berenguela?' she asks, curious.

'She is the new girlfriend of Isodore.'

'And who is Isodore?'

She is rather puzzled now, with all this new information.

'Isodore is my neighbour, who owns the bicycle repair shop next to the corner of the canal. He helps to keep me alive.' She does not understand this last bit of information. Her mind is somewhere else. Tomorrow is very far away and she can't wait and endure all this uncertainty. She must not lose her comb. Her precious comb, which belonged to the ancient queen of Granada, Spain. She can't risk it by waiting for something to happen. She must find a quick way to rescue her precious comb and suddenly she whispers, 'Aleppo! Chief, Aleppo!'

'The film is not done and the show must go on!'

6

Déjà Vu

The Chief sounds annoyed.

'What can we do about Aleppo? There is a war going on and that is not going to stop soon. Those poor refugees cannot be helped. The game is too big for anyone to understand. Those Middle Eastern countries have too many precious things and somebody wishes all those priceless objects to be erased completely. A nation is destroyed when it does not possess any cultural heritage. They must not have any history. They may have only a tiny little something, a lot less than a Mickey Mouse.'

But she pays no attention to what he says. She does not understand it anyway. She has been thinking very fast and starts breathing heavily.

'Chief, have you ever climbed the roof?'

'No. I have not. And you should not do that

either. Not because it is dark now. In daylight, it will be even more dangerous. The invisible 'them' will call the police and you'll be put in a psychiatric institution for the crime of committing suicide. Which is not allowed here.'

The Chief laughs a bitter smile.

'Chief, please help me open this window. I don't see much in the dark.'

She is pleading to him in a panicking tone. He opens the window for her and a cold wind blows into the room, taking away all the warmth they had produced earlier. She pushes her slender body half out of the window and whispers, 'Aleppo! Aleppo.'

The Chief hears a little coded knock on the wall and the creaking sound of an old window opening. There are whispers and little laughs are audible. Then she whispers, 'Thank you so much, dear Aleppo. Bless you.'

And then to him, 'Chief, please help me with this bag.'

There is a medium-size canvas sports bag in his hands, which is not very visible inside the room. She almost snatches the bag from him, holds it to her chest, kisses it loudly and then puts it on the floor. She is trying to find something in it. A few seconds later, she whispers in a joyful tone, 'Mumsy! Mums, I have it. It is not lost. I have got it, my mumsy!'

Whatever that was, he has no understanding of it. He needs to sleep, to pass the cold night. He will be waiting for the night to pass and the next morning, he will go to his only friend, Isodore. Perhaps he should not really call him a 'friend' of his. Isodore is more a shelter, who helps him to continue his search. The search he has been busy with, even though no-one yet knows what exactly he has been searching for.

She is happy but at the same time she is shivering with cold. He senses her discomfort and says, 'Tomorrow I'll go to Visigoth to fetch your clothes.'

'But I don't have any other clothes than these,' she says, as if she is surprised. He does not seem to be surprised. He is not the only one who has nothing. Perhaps they are two people brought together by the great force of the universe, because destiny had destined for them to be two destitutes under one roof.

She continues, 'You see, Chief, inside the

basements, it is kept very hot. Our working dresses are rather minimal. That is why it is very hot in there. And I am not allowed to go out, except to stand at the front door. So why spend money on clothes that would have no use in life?'

She says it right and he knows it right to his heart. No, clothes are not necessary for everyone. Unless one needs clothes to be someone.

But now they both feel that they need something to wrap their bodies to preserve their body heat. The roof has no insulation and the room feels rather chilly. She takes off her almost-black rubber boots and goes to sit on one corner of the sofa, beckoning to him to sit on the other side. He pulls the smelly blanket over them and covers her elegant and small bare feet with it. Her feet must not be cold, he thinks. My feet should not get cold, she thinks.

They try to close their eyes and not think of the unusual day that has gone by and not even daring to think what the next day will be like for them.

But that too has passed. It is a cloudy morning with drizzly rain, which has been dripping outside on the thin glass window panes. There is no clock to check the time. And they cannot see the street, because the room is at the back of the house. Both of them are feeling cold and both of them are trying to ignore it. They need to go somewhere where there is warmth, a place where they can use a toilet. A handful of warm water to clean their faces. And some food! Asking for a warm cup of coffee or tea will be more than a luxury. But a toilet and some food.

She could, of course, go to one of those coffee shops and ask them for a favour. After all, they are neighbours and they have shared their views often enough on her basement beds. But that was the paid life that she was thinking of. There is no room for charity in that world of buying and selling. She simply has no money to go inside those cafés and buy a cup of coffee.

They both look at each other as if they want to ask, 'How come you got no cent in your pocket?'

She looks down at her bare feet and his eyes follow hers. What beautiful feet those are! He could buy the most beautiful silk socks for her, for any price, if only he could afford to do so.

Now she is busy covering her feet with her woollen socks. And in a woolly sort of soft voice, she says, 'I don't have any money, Chief. I wanted to be the best of the best in this profession and I did make loads of bucks. But I have got nothing. You see, I did not keep any for myself.'

Before he can say anything, she continues, 'I know, no one will ever understand it. I had to give it all away. I had so much trouble. I had my ancestral village to take care of. You see, those people have always prayed for my well-being. They prayed for me when I was born. And they prayed for me when I was ill. They were there with me, while I was studying to become a doctor.'

'They never left me on my own. And, in return, I also promised never to let them be on their own. I made a vow that one day, after my studies, I was going to make loads of money and would take care of all of them! I would make my village happy by taking away their poverty. I wanted to give each of them a brand new prosperous life. I almost made it. But now this had to happen.'

She puts her boots on, covering the lower legs of her old jeans. An amber-coloured thin jacket covers her greyish T-shirt. Her thin body has no jewellery, nothing. She makes herself ready to go out. He feels relieved that she does not look at him and ask him about his own story. She does not and he thanks her in his mind.

Now they look at each other and see they are both extremely thin. Both of them think they will eat a lot when the time will permit them. Time is something that they both have to wait for. They both sigh at the same time, thinking time will bring it all to them.

She goes out first and he follows her. They both feel a kind of warmth inside their chests, which says, 'We are not alone!' She shakes her hands and her left hand goes behind her, where his right hand has been waiting to hold hers. Their hands meet and a sense of togetherness fills their hearts again. They go down the street, hand in hand, and look around. Then they start walking, just like the others, who have everything. Well, almost everything.

They walk to the end of the street and after taking a turn, they come to a corner where there's an old bicycle shop. The shop is defending its privacy with a huge ancient wooden door, with huge iron knobs attached to it. One really needs lots of strength to push that door open. The Chief pushes the door open and lets her go inside first.

He enters after her and feels the warmth on his thin cheek. She looks at him and, with his finger, he points at a corner which is covered by an old thick cotton curtain, printed in wild rose petals. She opens the curtains and the pungent stink of stale urine hits her nose. She wants to run away. But she does not.

After she has come out from behind the curtains, she finds the Chief having a conversation with an elderly white lady. Her fingers are without any rings, giving an impression that she does not enjoy any bondage with any other person. Her hands bear the marks of hard work and her eyes show sleeplessness. Altogether, she looks so tired, as if she needs rest and a long, silent sleep, she thinks, as she moves toward them.

The Chief smiles at her and says, 'Beren, this is Pos. She used to be our neighbour. But now she is out of her job. And she needs some warm clothes.'

Posette looks at Beren and says, 'Actually, we don't need clothes. We just need a little blanket. The Amsterdam nights are so chilly.'

Beren comes near to shake her hand and introduces herself in a regular sort of way, saying, 'I am Berenguela. It is a name from Granada, Spain.'

Posette shivers! Is that her hungry stomach which is giving her a kick? Is that a dream? A nightmare! She has heard this name before! She certainly has. There is no mistake about that. She remembers a Berenguela playing a musical instrument resembling a piano, so divinely. Now she is watching her fingers. Her fingers are full of the marks of hardship and her short fingernails still contain some tiny bits of flour. She must have been kneading dough this morning to bake something in her own oven.

Berenguela opens her cane-basket and a stomach-aching smell of freshly baked bread hits their noses. She gestures to them to sit down around a metal table that is standing in a corner of the place with a couple of broken plastic chairs around it. As if the cane-basket has magical power, the old and dirty table fills up with bread, cheese and of course homemade butter. There is also a pot of jam, shining in its glass jar like a piece of amber.

There is a damaged electric kettle, half hidden under a broken wheel. The Chief takes it behind the rose printed curtain to fill it up with some water from the tap and, again, a gust of stink hits their nostrils.

The water is boiled and the Chief makes tea in used paper cups. As they are sitting around the table eating the delicious bread, suddenly the huge wooden doors creak and a large shadow leans over them. A very tall and broad guy looks at them and says, 'Ah, I would love a cup of coffee.' The Chief hands him a paper cup and says, 'Pos, this is Isodore. And Isodore, this is Posette.' Posette looks at the guy. Her eyebrows arch, as if she is trying to recall something.

This very tall guy is unshaven and untidy. His beard is hanging from his face like hawthorns. In exactly the same way, his hair is hanging like brown wet hay, stacked in a bare field. His dark coloured T-shirt is not large enough to cover his wide chest. His white face is looking brownish. Probably he has also worked hard in the cold wind. These are hard-working people, she thinks. She used to know a world like that once, where hopefully they don't have to toil so hard anymore. Hopefully! Yes, she has always kept hope inside her chest.

Isodore comes to her and extends to her his large hand for a friendly shake. He says, 'You look very different behind the window, hey?' She smiles awkwardly and the Chief comes to her rescue.

'Pos is a doctor too, Isodore.'

'Oh! Is that so?'

Now he really shakes her hand cordially but

Posette pulls her hand away from him.

She keeps staring at him in such a way as if she has met her arch-enemy from many centuries ago. She is shaking her head. The Chief comes to her and says, 'Pos, what has happened?'

Isodore smiles a shy smile and says, 'Never mind me mentioning the windows. It was just a joke. Beren always says I don't have a sense of humour. I am so sorry.'

Posette looks at him and shivers. Who is this guy? And who does he resemble? She is sure that she has never met him before. He has never been one of her customers. Why does he make her feel so unwell? She goes to sit in the far corner of the room, where broken pieces and parts of bicycles are piled up. She looks around the place. It is huge in surface.

From outside, its size is hardly imaginable. But it is huge. It is very, very big. High above, a glass roof is fixed with the old wooden roof, letting lots of light through. In that daylight, a bicycle can be seen hanging from chains, upside down, as if a patient is lying on the operating table in a hospital. It all makes her shiver.

Then she looks around the floor and the

corners. Under a pile of old junk bicycle wheels, which are almost covered by a greasy plastic sheet, she sees something gleaming. She goes closer to it and tries to remove the plastic cover. The four legs of a wooden object become visible. She makes a gesture to the Chief. But Isodore answers, 'That is a huge piece of furniture. Someone left it here many years ago. He was going to come back and pick it up. But so far, he has not. Maybe one day, he will make time for it.'

Suddenly another shadow comes in. The Chief pours a paper cup of tea and Beren cuts a slice of bread from a loaf. The shadow sits down on one of the stools and looks around.

'How are the streets, Marco? Are the police busy chasing you guys from the streets?' Berenguela asks politely.

Marco is looking at his torn plastic bag, which says it belongs to Dirk van de Broek supermarket. He has been searching for something but probably he could not find anything. Now he is eating his bread, sopping it in the warm tea. He seems incredibly happy looking at Posette, who is gazing at something.

A vagabond who lives on the streets should not

look at a lady like that. That's what is on Isodore's mind, who says to Marco, 'Huh, Marco, Beren needs some help on her farm. You see, Ivan is sick. And I am very busy here.' Marco probably does not hear what Isodore is saying to him. His eyes are fixed on the incredibly thin and bare fingers of Posette, as if he feels a great disappointment at seeing her reach for something that she can't get hold of.

She has drawn herself even nearer to the shiny metal objects and says, 'May I see what it is?'

She says it in such a fearful tone that the Chief goes to help her. He pulls the heavy, greasy plastic away for her. This reveals a huge wooden musical instrument, looking extremely old and resembling a piano. The Chief opens its cover. There is some gold lettering which reads, 'Dresden, Germany'. The year or date of its making has disappeared.

Suddenly there is a noise and they all see Posette lying on the floor, her mouth agape. Her eyes are wide open with unfathomable fear. She is mumbling something like, 'The Dresden Piano!'

'The film is not done and the show must go on!'

7

The Crying Wall

She hears the hissing sounds of rough winds, hitting the top of the windows as if thousands of dragons have woken up after thousands of years of unconscious sleep, to catch up with her, as if they have an old quarrel to settle with her. Or is that the sound of the waves under the ocean, passing through a capsized boat?

She is trying hard to understand her situation. She feels warm, as if she has been wrapped up by a thousand pieces of fur-coats. Perhaps some posh mink or something much warmer than that. What could be warmer than that? The fur coat of the Tsarina of the Romanov dynasty? Or perhaps a wrapper of the fashionable Catherina the Great?

'I never had a fur coat. I could have bought it though. But I did not dare to! Luxury and comfort were not meant for me.'

Why should anyone need a fur coat for that matter?

She is asking herself in her dreams, while thousands of dragons are hissing outside. That must be it! The fire of the dragons' mouths is keeping her warm. 'Thank you, dragons,' she murmurs, 'thank you, I have been so cold all the time. I wanted to wear a teal coloured woollen sweater. I wanted to sleep under an old rose quilt and two soft pillows, made of white duck feathers. And those two pillow covers are matched with the cover of the quilt. The same old roses, whose petals will be kissing me on the face fondly, to say goodnight! But he did not let me. That wanton guy!'

Now she hears voices and arguments. A deep male voice is suggesting something to someone and a female voice is answering him in a very strange sort of way. Her voice is so familiar to her! She feels a squeeze in her tummy. The querulous female voice rises up and down.

'You know – I don't do banks and I don't do emails. And I hate the internet. That Bill Gates guy, why did he have to upset my world? Who told him to invent all that rubbish?'

'Yeah, but Beren, this is the world we live in now. In this modern life, you need a bank account and you need an internet connection to have access to be able to read your email. Trust me, you'll like it. And there are things like Facebook, Twitter and Instagram, which will help you to make friends in every corner and alley of this planet. Internet connection will bring the whole world into your living room.'

The male voice produces a small laugh.

But she does not laugh. Her voice sounds sad as she says, 'Iso, I don't want the world in my living room. How can someone be my friend, if I have never met them in reality? Or a person who could never come to sit next to me, to hold my hand, in pain or joy? What am I going to do with the whole world? Let the world be where it is now.'

Her sobbing continues. 'I want my four faithful seasons around my farm. I want a snow-covered winter. I want the spring to be full with new born calves. I want the summer growing bright with wheat and flowers. I want autumn to bring rest in our farm. Where we were born and grew up. Where our parents passed away peacefully and left us behind to continue. Here in this place, I want to live and die and my little brother will live forever!'

Now she hears a devastated cry.

Brother! Some lady is crying for her brother. Did she ever have a brother too? Or a mama? Was there anyone to love her? To cry for her? Suddenly someone starts to cough an unstoppable cough and she can guess the serious condition from the sound of it. She has a little moment of surprise that she has been sleeping under a well-made flowery quilt. And she has two pieces of black and white striped clothes on her. Those, they call a set of 'pyjamas'. But now she has no time to focus on her apparel.

She follows the sound and finds the source of it next to the room where she has been sleeping. There is a small single bed next to the wall, facing the window. The colour of the white curtains matches the off-white wall paint. She opens the curtains and a gloomy daylight comes in. Then she turns. A very thin guy is on the bed, sitting propped up against a couple of odd-sized pillows.

Another fit of coughing makes his body bend over. She goes to him and sits next to him. Her hand starts rubbing his back with her tiny, soft fingers. Slowly he bends down and his head is resting on her chest. She continues rubbing his back softly to make him calm, like a mother comforting her ill child.

Suddenly many footsteps are heard on the staircase and couple of heads peer inside. Among them, she can only recognise Berenguela, Isodore and the Chief. The Chief! What is wrong again? Where is she? Who are all those people? They are all watching her in a peculiar gaze and she looks at herself. She is dressed in oversized men's pyjamas and her feet are bare. She has nothing further to cover her slender body.

And there is a sick and wan man, whose head is hanging on her chest. His weak hands are slacking around her, holding her like a sailor from a capsized boat in the middle of the sea, hanging on to a piece of thin plank, fighting for his life, floating on the surge.

Slowly she puts down the head of the ill man on his pillow and covers him with his white quilt. The ill man's hands slacken to let go of her body and he starts searching for it again, as if a baby is searching for its mother in its worst nightmare. She puts one hand on his chest and with the other hand she starts to caresses his forehead and his hair.

Maybe when he was a healthy young boy, his

hair was golden and full of curls. Now his bare forehead looks rather large and his thin hair does not cover his skull evenly. But his greenish-blue eyes are very much alive as if he is ready to tell the story of a singing mermaid.

'His name is Ivan and he is my little brother. I'll spend my last coin to save his life. Do you understand that?'

She looks at the direction of the voice and Berenguela is standing there. She is wearing a black house-coat. She is hardly visible. As if she is not there. Perhaps her cloak makes her invisible, as if there is only a ghostly voice present there, without a figure. Her mind starts to move forwards and backwards. She does not recollect many of the things that have happened. She met some people in the bicycle shop where she was horribly frightened by something. There was the Chief watching her. After that, she has no remembrance of anything.

She looks at the Chief, who is standing in the far corner of the room. She feels dizzy and cold. She looks outside and she can see the surges of the rough sea crawling like a thousand snakes dancing together to make the end of this world. The wind is churning the roof of the house. Is she going through an unstoppable nightmare? Is this all real? Where is she? She feels the need to wake her brains and work out her condition.

'Pos, we are in Beren's house. Yesterday morning you passed out in Isodore's bicycle repair shop. We had to bring you here. We had no choice. We did not dare to bring you to a hospital. We did not know whether you had health insurance or not. The worst scenario is that you might not have a work permit or a stay permit for that matter. So, we took you here in Beren's van and she has put you in bed. But now as you can see, Ivan is deadly ill.'

She does not know what to say. She looks at sleeping Ivan and puts her index finger on her lips, gesturing to the others not to make any sound. She shushes the ill man now, who closes his eyes and has fallen totally into the arms of tranquillity. Then she looks at Beren and says, 'Don't worry, Beren. We all will take care of him. All of us together will bring him to the other world. You see, the other side is not so bad. The universe has arranged it all for us. Have faith in the cosmos. It will be alright again.' She looks at the Chief, who smiles and says, 'The film has not ended yet and the show must go on!'

'There is a little toilet in the corner of the attic, which we made for Ivan. But downstairs, you'll find the real bathroom and a larger toilet. The pyjamas that you are wearing belong to Ivan. I am going to find some clean clothes for you.'

Berenguela moves towards the staircase and Posette looks at the Chief.

He seems choppy and at the same time unusually thoughtful. He looks at Posette, makes a mysterious gesture and says, 'The Old Man above has fixed every bit for us. So why worry?' He says it in such a way as if he is saying goodbye to his bride. Then he follows Berenguela out of the room.

Posette also follows them downstairs to find the bathroom and she is rather surprised to see it. It is a large room, decorated with fancy things like the boudoir in their basement working place. There is a beautiful set of commode, bidet, washing-basin, heated towel racks and large gilded mirror. Several new toothbrushes are on the rack, different brands of toothpastes standing alongside.

There are a couple of new combs of different colours and sizes. And in the corner, there is a brand new little white bath! Is she dreaming all of this? The bath is running. It has already been filled up with lukewarm water. Some bath salts are creating some foam on top of it. She wants to jump into the suds and sit in it for hours.

But there is a knock on the bathroom door which startles her. She opens the door slightly to see a woman handing her some clean white towels and some ladies' clothes, which smell soothing from conditioner, well ironed and neatly folded. The woman says, 'I have made the bath ready for the master. But he is not well today. What a waste of the lovely warm water. You may have a bath, if you wish.'

The woman leaves her alone in a dream world. She has never had a bath in her whole life. Now, she does not know where she is. And there is a white bath waiting for her to lie down in its warm scented water! Is it real? Does she dare to put her smallish feet in that water and sit in that little white bath after all?

So she does. And when she gets out of the bath and puts on the clothes, she does not know who she is. The clothes are old-fashioned, a long-sleeved skirt with a petticoat sewn inside it. The colour of its blue and yellow printed flowers has faded quite a bit over the years. But it fits her well. That lady must have been about her size. She looks at her high blond hair which she has cut short because of her job. In this new outfit, she can't imagine anybody forcing her to wear a dark haired wig on her head.

Coming out of the bath, she feels extraordinarily clean and she thinks she has known this place all along. She goes into the kitchen, where all of them are waiting. No one says a word. A large oak table is laid. There are at least twelve chairs around it and all of them are occupied except one at the head. That could be the chair for the lady of the house?

She sits on it and suddenly a mild ray of sunshine falls on her. The little printed flowers on her garments smile too. Everybody looks outside through the window and they all have a smile on their faces. The sun is shining after all. There will be a sunny day to work.

After a hard morning's work, they have all returned for lunch. The table is laid. Warm soup bowls are steaming. Home baked loaf is being sliced. Dark brown cheese is shining like amber pieces shine in the mine. There is marmalade in a jar, strawberry jam in a little bowl, buttermilk in a cool jug. Heated milk and cold milk in large bowls.

Drinking glasses and large glass cups, everything is laid as perfectly as it should be.

When Berenguela goes up the stairs to check on her brother, she finds him in a clean pair of pyjamas, his face shaven, two pillows under his knees. He is half sitting against the wall, showing the comfort of the whole world. Posette is feeding him soup from a yellow little bowl with a silver spoon. They do not even look at her. She leaves the two of them quietly without making any noise. Maybe she also has a smile on her wry sad face.

When Berenguela comes down, the Chief gazes at her intensely and says, 'Beren, your brother will live forever. Please save all you have for him. He is going to need it.' She has a vague look on her face.

'Now, I hope you are not going to need me here. I have to go now.'

And he leaves, saying farewell to everybody. Only he does not ask for Posette to take his leave. Goodbyes are not necessary between them, he thinks. But what he doesn't know is that that farewell was to return to that place the very next day.

'The film is not done and the show must go on!'

8

Au Revoir

He is walking along the narrow grassy path, when an orange-coloured old van stops at his side and the driver says, 'Want to enjoy a ride, mister? Getting kind of lonely behind the wheel all by myself. Going to the city to bring some fresh veggies for some fancy restaurants, you know.'

He does not even look at the driver but goes to sit next to the driver's seat. The driver prattles on endlessly but he remains mute. It looks sunny and the sunlight is somehow bothering him.

'Do we need so much light for ourselves?'

In fact the talkative driver asks him that question and he nods his head in an ambiguous way.

The van driver has stopped somewhere, and makes an excuse to him, telling him he needs a bit of time to empty his bladder and it is really the fault of the diabetics tablets that he has been swallowing, diabetic type two, which is beyond control. He wants to say that he used to know an amazing doctor, who could cure any disease in no time.

And that was a nice little Polish girl, who possessed the most beautiful pair of feet on this planet. She was a doctor, who had been sold to a devil and her name is Posette. But he has lost her now in a wilderness and he will never find her address again. He also gets out from the orange mini-van, along with the driver, who is a type two diabetic patient.

Dusk has fallen when he arrives at his one-room apartment. The narrow staircase to the top floor seems very tiring to climb. He feels he has never done it before. He starts to question himself, 'Why do I live here? Who am I? What am I searching for?'

He had a very simple lock on his door which he now finds open. He has nothing and everyone in the neighbourhood knows it. Who wants to rob a place which does not have even a toilet? He opens the door, goes inside and collapses on his sofa-bed.

He feels tired, sick and angry. He looks around

and sees a bag, a faded purple little bag. Oh! Posette's bag! Now, what to do? She must be worrying about that special thing which she had from her mother. But he can't bring her the bag now. He must give it to Isodore. But he is long gone home. Maybe he will bring it to her by himself. Maybe Berenguela will come tomorrow morning and maybe she could give him a ride. Or maybe she does not need those childhood things anymore, now that she has got a new life. A perfect life for her, the life of a farmer's lady!

But whatever he may think, a strange kind of loneliness is creeping through his heart. He was not aware of these kinds of feelings before. The whole place seems so empty. Only the remaining pieces of her memory are lingering in the cold air. He wanted to lie down and have a dreamless sleep. But the loneliness is hurting him like a sharp knife cutting his vein. He picks up the bag and looks inside it. There is nothing in it to hold on to. He gets angry and throws away the bag on the floor. A very strange-looking comb-like wooden thing falls out. He goes to pick it up and sees a photograph lying next to it, upside down. With a heart full of hope, he turns the photo. He wanted to see her face again.

Instead, he sees a picture of an unknown place. It is a photo of a place surrounded by mountains. The green lush valley is decorated by some white patches of snow. Clear fountain water is jumping down below and running into a large green lake. Some little white houses are spread across the valley. Some domestic animals are grazing. A little fairy child is holding a baby deer on her lap and suckling it with a milk bottle.

It must be a picture of some part of a heaven, he thinks. He turns the photo over and sees something written in English, in a child's hand. It says, 'The Ghwarband valley of Afghanistan, the Yousufzai tribe of Pushtoon.' What a picturesque place that is, he thinks. Or perhaps, it is a photograph of a painting. Sometimes painters try to create something like a heaven, from the image of their own imaginations.

He looks at the photo again and suddenly he feels as if someone else is also looking at the photo with him. But he feels too tired to turn around. He looks at the photo of the old Chief of Arizona, hanging on the wall. On normal days, he would have a long conversation with his grandfather. But today, he feels nothing. He does not even have the heart to say to the photo that he has not yet found the thing he has been searching for. He sits down on his sofa-bed and closes his eyes. He feels lonely. Very much alone on this earth. If only he had someone to talk to. If only there was someone to hold his hand, as she did some time ago!

It is completely dark inside his room now and he closes his eyes. A heavenly voice is touching his senses of hearing and in a soft voice it says, 'Are you cold?' He does not dare to open his eyes. He does not want his dreams to be broken. He utters in a murmur, 'Yes. I am so cold.' Then he feels his body is being covered by his dirty old blanket. The same sweet voice is saying again, 'Are you thirsty?' He nods. 'Yes!'

He feels a little bottle in his hands and drinks some of it. It has a strange taste. It is a kind of sweet drink. Perhaps it also comes from heaven. Perhaps they make such drinks for those who are lucky enough to possess a seat there.

'Are you a bit hungry now?'

Now he did not feel comfortable any more.

The angelic voice has gone too far. No. No. He never gets hungry. He knew it from his mother's womb that he will never be hungry. He recalls every single thing since he was created and was given a soul, while he waited inside the velvety womb of his mother. He was not hungry while he waited for his mother to come home and feed him. Only once, yes, that was only one time he was sad and upset.

He was probably three or four months old then. His mother had to go somewhere on some urgent business and someone else was there to give him a bottle of milk. A bottle of milk was ready there for his hungry little tummy. But he refused to drink that. He wanted his mother's milk. And nothing else.

Finally his mother came back at the end of the day, exhausted from a long bus trip. Her breasts were swollen with milk, which had collected throughout the day. But when she returned to her baby and wanted to feed him, her breasts were hard and the milk would not flow. She felt pain and he had cried a sad cry. He was upset and his crying curved lips made it clear that he had missed his mother.

She knew it and she whispered into his ears, 'I'll never leave you alone, dear one!' He believed her.

Then he was quiet and sucked peacefully and sweet milk was running again through his mother's soft little nipples.

How wonderfully he slept that night, lying on the fair and slender left arm of his mother. His mother sang the lullaby, which he already knew by heart while sleeping in her womb. He had chosen his mother all by himself, while his soul had been searching for a place to rest. And secretly taken shelter in her, only to surprise her later. He wanted to wait till he could pronounce words like, 'Maman, I am your wish, now lying on your chest!' Did he say that to her? Did he utter those words to her? He is trying very hard to remember.

'No, dear fairy, no. I am never hungry. My stomach is full with my mother's milk,' he says wearily. The smiling fairy says, 'That was a long time ago. Then you were a baby?'

'Yes, fairy dear. As a baby you learn a lot. I had to learn all of it for myself. My mother did not know that I had already chosen her as my mother. So she did not have the chance to teach me much. But I knew it all. I knew dirty guys, who made wagers to see her breasts.'

There was a lot of money at stake. The bet was

that she would open her blouse for her hungry crying baby. And that wanton drug addict villain who had set up that abetment, had locked the door from outside, so that his mother could not go out with him. Those thugs had lived wallowing in sin and they came into his mother's room pretending to view the new baby.

The wantons were sitting opposite his mother for hours, so that the baby would cry and she would be forced to open her blouse to feed him. But he knew it. And his mother knew it. So he did not cry for half of the night. And when they finally left, he opened his twinkling bright eyes, which met his mother's salty face. He slept the whole night on his mother's beautiful skinny chest and he promised himself that he would never embarrass his mother by crying for food.

He recalls that horrific event every time hunger churns his flat tummy and he says, 'My tummy is carrying the amulet of my mother's milk.' That amulet creates an analgesic effect, both physically and mentally. He feels as if he is flying towards some known place now.

The fairy produces a sad laugh and says, 'I know a lot about that. But wait, there is someone coming up the stairs. It must be Visigoth. He must not see me here. Close the window behind me.' He hears his window open and a gust of cold wind bruises his face. He opens his eyes and his door creaks.

A tall figure is standing in front of him. He gets up but before he can say anything, the tall figure demands an answer. 'Where is Cher? Why is your room so dark?' He goes to the open window and checks outside.

'Now, Chief, I swear by every little unborn child, that I'll find that slut and I'll make her bones suffer for it. You better bring her to me. Otherwise, I'll make you mashed potatoes.'

Visigoth tries to turn on the light. But he realises that there is no bulb in its socket. He looks around the room like a hound and says, 'I know she was here. I can almost smell her. You cannot hide her from me. You must bring her back before I find her.' Visigoth checks the open window again and kicks the door before leaving.

He does not bother closing the door nor the window. He just keeps sitting on the sofa, hoping someone will clothe him with something warm. Cold wind is coming through the window and passing through the door. He is so tired. He does not care. He keeps his eyes closed and his mind flies away to a place he so much longs for.

Then he starts feeling more comfortable. It is not so cold anymore. His body feels warm. A tiny arm is wrapped around his thin body. His window is closed and so is his door. Then he even smells some bread. His stomach rumbles. He has not had anything for many hours now. The tiny hand puts something in his mouth and he chews the pieces of bread.

The same hand gives him a bottle of drink and he drinks the sweet drink. He feels so comfortable now. He has eaten and he has had a sweet drink. He is not cold anymore. He is not alone anymore. There is a little fairy who is keeping watch over him. He has a happy smile on his thin dry lips and he says, 'It's okay, *maman*. One day, we'll meet again.' As if he is going back to his dreams.

When he opens his eyes much later, he is shocked to see a little fairy lying on his bare wooden floor, her head resting on her arm, wrapped up in a green velvet skirt and purple blouse, with a large yellow shawl around her neck. A bit of early morning light is coming through the window and that has fallen on top of her. He looks at the little figure. It is a chrysalis waiting to bloom like a chrysanthemum! The little figure opens her emerald green eyes, which meet his. He remains on his sofa, flabbergasted.

She smiles at him and says, 'We have no time to sit here. Visigoth will be here soon. He is searching for Cher. That apish man has given him a load of money to find her. And I don't want to go back there either.'

'But who are you? How did you come here?'

He was still in his dreams.

'I came here through the window, climbing the roof from the window next door. But let's hurry.'

She takes Posette's purple bag in her hands and pushes her shawl inside it. Then she takes off her skirt and blouse. Under them are some thin dark leggings and a T-jama. She puts her clothes in the bag too. Then she picks up the dirty blanket and wraps herself with it from head to toes.

'Come on, Chief. We must hurry before he catches us. It is still dark outside and it is time for them to sleep.'

Soon they are on the streets. They walk very fast, hand in hand. The city is still asleep and they have to find a way to reach Posette, who is in danger now. They have to find transport. A bus is making itself ready to move. But he has no money to buy a bus ticket.

There are some homeless vagabonds sleeping under a shed. She goes to examine one of them and very quickly she returns and says, 'How much do we need for a bus ticket?' She shows some big coins and paper notes in her hands.

'Who are you?'

He sounds very surprised and scared at the same time.

'I am Aleppo. The famous thief of the valley of Pushtoon of Ghwarband. I belonged to the clan named Yousafzai.'

'Thou shalt not steal. Go and return that money to the poor man,' he commands her with a rough voice. She starts pleading, 'But look, Chief, that man does not need so much money and he will earn some more in no time! We are fugitives and we are on the run. And of course, we can return the money to him anytime. Believe me, Chief, I know how to earn honest money. I am much, much better than Cher in that business.'

His hand feels hard on her tiny fair cheek before both of them realise what is happening.

She does not cry. She does not protest against his act. She goes back to the homeless guy and says something, handing him back his money. He is watching the scene and he can see that the ragged old guy is putting back his money in her small hands, including some more, which he has found searching the various pockets of his ripped old coat. And she is saying to him, 'Thank you, Simon. It will not be long before your luck will change. I'll do that for you. You can't live forever on the streets! Bye, dear Simon.'

A van stops near them, braking hard. It produces a screeching sound that hurts the ear, as if the tyres are grinding into the road surface. He turns back and sees the face of that prattling driver, who is beckoning to them to get into the van quickly, because he is not allowed to park here. As soon as they jump in, the driver starts to talk with her.

They are on the highway in no time and he asks her, 'So, you two are alone, hey? Has the mother run away?' He gives a hearty laugh about his own joke.

'No. My mother did not run away. I did.'

Her voice is calm as the morning cold. They are sitting next to the driver's seat and now she has laid her head on the Chief's lap. She feels so sleepy as she says, 'You see, I have to find my lost husband.'

Probably the driver cannot take the joke anymore. His beer-belly is hanging out from his black T-shirt and jeans. After a while, he stops at exactly the same place where he stopped last time, to empty his bladder, which fills up rather fast because of his type-two diabetes. The Chief gets out too with the little girl and the driver advises him, saying, 'Hey you, be very careful with that little girl of yours. She is much too smart for her age. I would talk to her mother, if I were you.'

He nods and she smiles.

Now they have to walk for a while. Maybe Aleppo is getting hungry. But he does not want to talk about it. He does not get hungry. But that little child! Why does the Old Man above always mix up his simple life with all these complicated matters? Hopelessness is creeping inside his chest now.

There is a small shady tree next to the road and a little rock is standing under it. Aleppo points at it and they go to sit there. Then she opens the purple bag and takes out some old pieces of smelly bread and a plastic bottle with coloured drink. 'This is all we have, Chief, for our breakfast. Then we'll have to see. Come, let's eat.'

Now he realises that last night, when his tummy was churning inside his abdomen with extreme hunger, these little hands were putting bread inside his mouth. That was the plastic bottle that contained some drink for his thirst. He shudders at the thought that this little fairy had been feeding him her own food and till now she has not eaten anything. An enormous shame makes him feel crippled. Why is he continuing his life? What for? What if he never finds it? And what exactly is he searching for?

The sun rises in all its glory, while they eat their bread and drink the drink from that plastic bottle. They see a big van passing by and a clergyman looks at them and smiles. Suddenly the Chief's right hand moves to his left side and he hold his chest in such a manner, as if his heart is going to come out from its cage.

Aleppo looks at his painful face and says, 'Let's move on, Chief. We must find Cher before the others do.'

'Yes, Aleppo. Let's try to find her.'

His legs want to run against the storm which is heading for him. But he can't even keep up with

Aleppo. She holds his hand in hers and says, 'Let's walk slowly. We are not in a hurry now, are we, Chief?'

They walk at a slow pace indeed. And so they arrive at the little wooden gate of Berenguela's farmhouse. There are some tables laid outside, in front of the house. The tables are covered with white cloths and each table has on it a vase with fresh flowers, coming from the back garden. The sweet smell of freshly baked cake is floating around. It is all beautiful and calm. A warbler is singing happily nearby. He feels he should not be here. He may not desecrate this holy place.

A wheelchair is coming out from the house. Ivan is sitting on it, wearing an old and shabby suit which is too large for him. A red tie is hanging from his neck. But his sickly looks are gone! He looks as if he is on his way to convalescence. Then out comes that clergyman whom they had seen on the way. Then, hurrying, out comes Berenguela, telling the priest that some Ucles will be late and so will Isodore. They will need someone else to give away the bride! And the housemaid, who was going to be the bridesmaid, has been ill from last night. The clergyman smiles and says, 'Ask Him for clemency.'

And there they are. Posette comes out from the house in an old white wedding dress, which looks off-white now. She has a lacy veil covering her head and face. Aleppo is holding her hand, acting as her bridesmaid. She has changed into her shiny green satin clothes now. How beautiful the little girl looks in her old traditional clothes! Aleppo brings the bride to the Chief and the bride holds his arm with all the trust in the world.

No voices are raised against this holy matrimony and the Chief gives the bride away. Keeping the Old Man as their witness, the clergyman pronounces them husband and wife. Posette pushes the wheelchair and they disappear inside the farmhouse.

'The film is not done and the show must go on!'

9

God-Forsaken Souls

Suddenly there is a gust of wind causing a whirring noise. Perhaps it is coming from the sand dunes nearby. He looks around. Berenguela is sitting at a table with the holy man and Aleppo is sitting in the corner table with the maid, who has been sick since last night. Aleppo is holding the maid's right hand with her left hand and nodding her head in all directions.

Sometimes she is nodding to her left. Then immediately to her right. Suddenly looking up and again down. A large silver fork is in her left hand, which she is using to nibble into an enormous strawberry cake, which is on a large golden plate, meant specially for a cake like that.

The maid now removes her hand from Aleppo's and dries her eyes and nose with a paper napkin.

With her now free hand, Aleppo moves the large cake towards her, using the fork as if it is a sword being used in the battlefield. She has started to attack the strawberry wedding cake vigorously.

He feels like the leftover carcass of a turkey, after the Christmas dinner. He walks backwards, trying to recall the scenario of the whole morning. The little wooden gate closes behind him automatically. Again he is on his way. He wanders through the sand dunes, along the bushy little paths. He is not in a hurry. He has no place to go. He can walk like this his entire life, like a wanderer. He can get himself lost in the vault of the sky.

There are incessant options for him. He could be a wandering bard. He could sing songs with dancing gypsies and could travel with them in their wandering caravans. That would not be a silly thing to do. Gypsies do not belong to any place and he does not belong to any one. His Gypsy mind is wandering constantly to so many unknown places. He often feels like a wandering bard about himself.

Again a whirring noise startles him out of his absent-minded reverie while an orange van stops next to him. Without waiting for an invitation, he opens the van's door and gets in to sit next to the driver's seat. The driver can't stop chatting. 'So, where is that little one? I must say that she is much too ripe for her age. But she is a very nice heart-warming little thing. Hey, you are lucky to have a precious thing like that. A girl. I always wanted to have many girls at my home. But you know, one has to be lucky to have those sorts of things in one's life. Instead I had four sons. They left with their mother.' The Chief does not react.

'I pay the alimony but they don't even want to see me. In the family court, they all said that they have a new father now and he is a very nice father for them. That new father does not work through the weekends and evenings; he is always at home. He takes the boys to play football and he cooks pasta for them. Which I could never have done. Because I am always in my van. My ex-wife's boyfriend has taken my home and my family and I am working day and night to pay for their comforts.'

He remains silent and uninterested. The van driver feels upset and looks at his fellow passenger and asks, 'Why don't you say anything? Don't you have any sympathy for people? Have you never lost anything?'

The driver has to stop at the same place, as his

type two diabetes is giving him a signal. He also gets out and starts to walk. He does not know how long he has walked, but in the end he comes to the Central Station. He sees the vagabond Simon, who smiles at him and says, 'Chief, where is that little elf? She is right, you know. My luck has already changed.' He shows a large moneybag and says, 'Just found it on the street.'

He says nothing.

Then he moves away. 'Hey Chief, I thought you were going to say, go to the police and hand it over to them. Aren't you?'

'It is all up to you, Simon.'

And he walks on. Simon looks at him from behind, nods his shaggy head and mumbles, 'Such a Chief! He could have been on the street like us. But his pride is keeping him away from such an unburdened free life!'

He doesn't care to know much, when and how he came to his home and got to the top floor. He doesn't bother to close his door or check his windows. He goes to sit on his sofa-bed and looks at the poster photo of the Chief of Arizona. He does not feel like having a conversation with him. He feels upset as he looks at the sharp eyes of the

Arizonian Chief, which are almost covered by crumpled skin and says, 'Why me? What have I done wrong?'

The old Chief remains quiet on his poster photo, as if he does not want to be disturbed. His two long, thick braids of dark hair are hanging down across both sides of his chest. Green and orange beaded golden ribbons are twisted through the thick, dark braid, making a shining zigzag design. His braids are gleaming like two poisonous snakes now, as if they are going to jump from his neck, and are planning to fly into his room, full of devious intentions. He shouts at him like a stubborn child. 'Don't you see that I am cold? Can't you just send me some warm wind from your side?'

His voice sounds full of despair.

He keeps looking at the poster of the Arizonian Chief, who is his grandfather. He looks at his shrunken eyes and the poster photo moves. The eyes of the Chief of Arizona laugh at him with unusual kindness and his old face smiles. Suddenly he feels warm air is blowing inside his room. He feels comfortable and goes to open his tap. Cold water flows on to his folded palms and he shivers. He drinks the cold water till his tummy cannot take any more. Now he feels relaxed.

He goes to sit on his sofa-bed again. He looks at his grandfather and he thanks him for being there, on the top of the Arizona Mountain. No matter how far the distance is, he has someone out there who can be reached, if necessary. After all, he has someone to call a blood relative. Genetic lines are so important for his clan and for himself. He needs a blood relation to feel alive.

But on the other hand, he almost had a family. He was about to have it all. He had her. She was right here, sitting next to him, sleeping on his sofa-bed. They had shared his only blanket. Oh! His blanket. He has not got that anymore. Aleppo has got it. She took it. Oh, dear Aleppo. That angelic child! She may have it. She may need that old blanket much more than he does. Let her have it.

Maybe one day, he will buy her a new blanket. A nice floral-pattern blanket, of the kind they sell in the open street markets. Probably they come from the Middle East or Turkey. They use brightly coloured flowery decorations. Western people do not need lots of colours. Westerners would rather keep everything simple and white. White makes it easy to come in and go out. After all, we have all always lived under the supremacy of the white world.

But who cares? He is not bothered by the colour of power. He is happy the way his brownish life has been. He has nobody, until he finds the one he is searching for. He lives on the top floor of a house, and has not paid the rent for a couple of months. There is cold running water there. There is no heating. But the sun shines in occasionally. And he had his old blanket, which is gone now.

Little Aleppo has got it. Let her have it. But he has left her behind! Yes he has. He has left behind all of it. For a fraction of a moment of his life, he had everything. There was 'she' and Aleppo. There were three of them. Having them around, his life was full. His sky-kissing luck seemed invincible. And now, a dark-hearted wizard has taken away all he loved. He loved his life for a drip of a moment. And that life has taken away his dreams of belonging to someone.

Someone was knocking on his door and becoming impatient, has come inside his room and saying, 'Since the door was open, I have invited myself in. But I have to run down again right away. My van is parked outside in a place the police are not going to be happy about. Sorry, can't stay for a cuppa. Got to run.'

He rolls his eyes. It was that prattling driver of that orange van. He has left two huge shopping bags on the floor. He gets up to close his door and looks at the biggest bag first and pulls out a nice-smelling blanket. It is his old stinking blanket, which has been washed, dried and folded with care. Then he looks in the other bag.

There are several small bags inside, which he pulls out one by one. There are several pieces of cake. The wedding cake! There is also bread, jam and butter. Finding two large candles and a matchbox makes him laugh. He must be dreaming. But why not eat the food, which the dream fairy has brought for him? He eats the bread and the cake.

Then he pulls out the blanket. Its nice smell makes him sleepy. He sits down on his sofa-bed. Then he gets up again to close his door, turning the key and leaving it in the door. Suddenly he feels he has valuables in his house and he needs to be careful. He has to protect all he has got in his life.

He goes to sit on his sofa-bed and he covers himself with his freshly washed blanket. He eats bread and cake. And he has some water to wash down all this nice food inside his tummy. Now he may sleep again. It is dark outside and the wind is whirling around like a naughty child. He feels like lighting a candle in his room, hoping to see one face. Or two faces!

He wants to thank them for the food they have sent him. He wants to thank the two fairies for their kindness and caresses. But he does not dare to. He does not dare to lose his dreams. He is afraid to ask about the practicalities of this implausible incident, like how did the van driver find him? From whom did he get his blanket? Who washed it and dried it for him? Who gave the bread? But why bother? Maybe none of it is real. Maybe when the night is over, these illusions will disappear too.

The sun is shining on his face and he wakes up. He looks around. Everything is the same in his room, except for the two plastic shopping bags lying about. There is still some bread and jam. And of course the wedding cake. And his old blanket, which has been cleaned with washing powder and scented fabric softener.

So it was not a hallucination after all. The van driver was here and somehow he knew where he lived. And someone had told the van driver to locate him and to bring things for him. He feels happy, even overjoyed. It does not matter much who that person is. But someone cares for him. And that's all that matters in life.

He washes his face with cold water and dries it with some of the paper napkins which were also in the plastic bag. Now he can have a breakfast as decent people have every morning. He eats, full of joy. Isodore must be there by now. He'll go to him now and do loads of work for him. That good soul Isodore. His back is hurting and the physiotherapist cannot do much for him. Painkillers have proven to be useless. And he can't afford to hire an assistant officially.

There are not many people nowadays anywhere who have a diploma or experience in repairing bikes. And if they do, they don't want to work really and to avoid it all together, they ask too much as wages, knowing that this man can't afford to hire them.

Vocational schools used to send their students to learn some repair works. But that also stopped a while ago. Mindless kids have got shiny iPhones in their hands. They are busy talking with friends who live at the other side of our planet and they take selfies. What is the fun of taking a photo of one's own face? And posting that on the so-called wall of a facebook? But this is a new-tech era that he has no knowledge of.

In fact, whether it is a technological era or not, Isodore cannot hire anyone. His bicycle repair shop does not make much money. Modern bicycles are rather complicated to fix. They are much more expensive than computerised cars and most of the parts are circuits and wires. Those modern bikes are more like machines than two-wheelers. Nobody wants to buy old bikes anymore.

People want fancy things. Kids want expensive things. Their parents have got such a lot of money nowadays to spend. They buy the newest things for their kids. Designer clothes are a must-have. It is a competitive society nowadays. The simplicity of life has gone undercover. Expensive clothes have decorated the fake faces. Names are changing, as well as the streets. Everything is being imitated, with nobody knowing what exactly is being copied and what good that is doing to us. Us? Does anybody care, how the 'us' are living nowadays?

The Chief lets go a deep sigh, as he thinks about

that great guy Isodore, whose life is miserable now because of all these changes in society.

Isodore's business is no longer doing well, even though he is still persevering with it. He loves his business and he can't imagine a life without fixing a bike. That is all he has done, since he was a kid. That has been the simple life of Isodore and he must help him. He must become the helping hand of Isodore. That Isodore, whom he so much likes to think of as a 'friend'.

'The film is not done and the show must go on!'

10

Simoom

He comes down only to find Visigoth sitting on the steps with a foreign-looking, smallish guy. He must be from Asia Minor. Or from South Asia perhaps. They both stand up on seeing him. The smallish guy looks at him with pleading, wet eyes but says nothing. Visigoth comes up to him as if he wants to rest one of his arms on his shoulder in search of some sort of comfort. But he does not.

Instead he says, 'Look, Chief, look at this guy. He is searching for her. It is not only for 'that' reason, if you know what I mean. This guy needs her. His job is at stake. He needs her and I need her. Please Chief, oh please, forgive me and bring her back. I miss her, Chief, I miss her!'

He looks at the two miserable guys and says in an indifferent tone, 'We all miss her. But she is not to be returned. As you must know, she is someone else's lawfully wedded wife now and will never return to anyone.'

'Married!'

The small guy collapses on the street and Visigoth sits down on the steps in total despair. He shows the utmost outrage and loudly shouts to the Chief, 'Wife? Lawfully wedded? Are you kidding me? Who in his right mind is going to marry a whore of Amsterdam? Hey? You are a lying son of a bitch. No wonder your mother left you. You are a trouble by birth. I wanted to throw you out of the house many months ago. But Lucretia, yes it was her, the queen of the whores, yes, she did not let me! Now does that surprise you? Hey?'

Lucretia! That majestic person had allowed him to stay in her house, which is rented to Visigoth? Why? He hardly ever sees her, let alone going near her. Why should she bestow such mercy on him! His room has nothing. It has no toilet and no heating in it. It is very cold most of the year. But it is a palace for him. He hardly pays anything for it. And it is perfect for him. He needs this location to continue his search. His search to find his own roots, which no one knows anything about.

Visigoth walks away, swearing at him in different languages. The small guy is still lying on the street, sobbing loudly like a hungry child who has lost his nanny in the crowd. He walks past him and heads for the corner of the street. He must help Isodore and Berenguela. He must never let them down. Because they have given 'her' a life.

Posette is now married to Ivan, Berenguela's terminally ill brother. Posette has an honourable home now and a respectable life. He feels appeased now, thinking that Posette possesses everything that she should have had much earlier and which, by some dark spell, did not happen until very recently.

And that little angel? Little Aleppo? Where is she? Visigoth has not mentioned her! Why? Didn't he notice that little Aleppo is missing too? Aleppo, that kind hearted, little angel. How he slapped her on her rosy cheek! He feels guilty.

'I must apologise to Aleppo, next time I see her. I must beg her for forgiveness.'

Isodore and Berenguela are already in their bicycle repair shop, when he arrives. They are drinking tea from old paper cups and are having a deep discussion. He comes out of the toilet and sits next to them with his cup of warm tea. He hears Berenguela saying to Isodore, 'Look, Iso, you are losing money in this business and I have practically no income from the farm. We need hired hands, which we can't pay for. We don't know enough people who can help us. We need experts and not just anybody. And nobody wants to be a bicycle mechanic or milkman nowadays. People have changed. Society has changed. What are we going to do to survive in this new ignorant world?'

He feels like a duffer, while listening to their conversation. He wants to say that he is there to help them all the way. But he hesitates. He does not know how to be brave enough to share the difficulties of the lives of these wonderful people. He has to prove nothing to them, only one thing that he is not a dunce, that he is capable of helping his friends.

If only he could call them his friends. Now Berenguela is talking about her home situation.

'Now that Ivan has a wife to take care of him, I have a lot more hours in hand. But still, I can't help you. I mean, what do I know of bicycles?'

This is the right moment to share his thoughts with them as the Chief says, 'I also don't know much about bicycles, Beren. But I know how to be a helping hand for honest friends. I'll be here, while you take care of your farm. Now show me please, where I begin. And oh, there is a guy, hanging around the Central Station, who is called Simon. Pick him up and tell him that a little angel wants to see him. He won't say 'no' to her.'

Berenguela looks surprised and he smiles at them.

'Just trust the Old Man above. The film has not ended yet. And the show must go on.'

So it does. Berenguela drives to the Central Station, where she sees a couple of police guys holding a vagabond with torn and shabby clothes. They have found a moneybag, full of large notes and bank cards of several banks, in his ripped coat pockets. The man seems rather vague about how he has found them.

In the meantime the police have called the owner of the wallet and a small Asian-looking guy arrives. He looks rather sad and, with an uninterested face, he thanks the police for finding his wallet. He does not want to press any charges against the vagabond guy called Simon. In fact he wants to give a reward to Simon for finding his wallet including its contents.

Berenguela goes to Simon and says she was sent here by a little angel to find him and bring him along with her. Simon goes to sit in her small farming-van without raising his eyebrows and they drive to her farm. When they arrive there, they find Aleppo busy stacking hay in the barn, together with a robust looking guy who looks at them sharply. He pushes his bushy ginger hair backwards, which uncovers his projecting forehead. It is very difficult to guess his age, because of his unshaven ginger beard. He could be thirty or he could also pass for fifty.

His ginger hair and chocolate brown eyes do not give away anything about him. His clothing and shoes are a sign showing that he has just jumped from a catalogue book. His appearance makes it clear that this guy has no reason to shop in a normal shopping street. There is a strange sort of air around him.

He has a curious smile on his face, when he introduces himself as Ucles de Seville, putting a lot of emphasis on the word 'Seville'. Apparently he is a journalist and looking for something very special. Aleppo has already hired him to find her lost husband, who is called Allah Shaheram of the Sherkhanzai clan!

Posette has been threshing grain, while Ivan is sitting in his wheelchair, watching his wife working. They look at each other and smile sweetly.

'Was he ever ill? Is he still dying?' Berenguela asks herself.

She looks at Ucles and asks what exactly has brought him here. He says in a heavy Spanish accent that he is a reporter. Of course he did not go to any college to train to be a reporter. He is self-taught and he likes to find lost things for people. He is a sort of one-man army, in the department of lost and found. He loves his job. And he especially loves those who hire him.

It has happened that one of his relatives, Jasmine of Seville, had hired him to find a musical instrument which had been lost at some point, centuries ago. The last time it was located was in a church in a small village in Poland. Then it was seen in Dresden, Germany. Probably, knowing the value of it, the German army had taken it to Germany. The latest news is that it was brought to Holland by a group of Gypsies. And now, coincidently, he has been hired by this little lady named Aleppo, who has lost her husband.

'How I love to find lost people!' He seems so amused by his own remarks.

'But how do you know where exactly a lost object is?' Brenguela asks in a calm tone.

'Aha. That is the job of a reporter. You see, they are better than any police detective. So far I have gathered that this unique piece is somewhere in a farmhouse, in a barn perhaps?' He looks directly into the eyes of Berenguela and she, looking at him, says sharply, 'So that is the reason that you are helping stacking hay in the barn? Did you find anything? There are thousands of farmhouses throughout Europe. How many have you searched?'

She seems upset.

So does Posette. When they are all sitting at the dinner table, she does not want to look at anybody. Ucles tries to start a conversation and says, 'So you are Posette. What an interesting name.'

Posette gestures to the maid that she needs help to bring Ivan back upstairs. But instead, Simon rises from the dinner table and takes Ivan in his arms. Posette looks at him once more and smiles.

Little Aleppo has already made this pot-bellied guy clean shaven and washed, putting him in old clean clothes of Ivan. It seems he is a strong middle-aged man. His shabby clothes and bearded face had made him look old. But he is not such an old guy after all. Little Aleppo has the kind-fairy's magic stick in her hands, which changes everything for the better.

Ucles watches them going upstairs. With a mysterious look, he says, 'And my dear, you are Berenguela? What a beautiful name! Where does this name come from, I wonder!'

His tone makes her irritated. She is now looking at Aleppo. She is a child of a bright light-dark complexion, which illuminates everything around her. A shiny child who knows her ways, who is so sure and self-possessed, as if she has everything under control. But what nonsense is she talking about? Hiring a stranger to find her husband! Or is that this strange guy, who is playing a practical joke on all of them?

She feels the urge to remove this guy out of their lives and says, 'Okay Ucles, the object you're searching for is not here. Now you may leave.'

'Leave?'

He almost utters a loud cry of despair.

'How can I leave without seeing Isidore? He

knows that I was coming to see him.'

'Well, he is Isodore, and not Isidore. He is busy somewhere else and he won't be free to come up here for a couple of days.'

She just does not like to look at him.

But he looks directly at her and says, 'Look, Berenguela, I am here to do some business and I have to meet Isidore de Seville! I must meet him, before it is too late! You need some help on your farm and I am here, who knows everything about farming life. You don't have to like me. But just hire me, as Aleppo has done.'

Berenguela seems very upset now and says, 'Aleppo, what nonsense is that? What is this rubbish story about finding a missing husband?'

'Oh! That is not a story! I lost my husband and I want to find him. So I hired Ucles. Because only a media man can do such things.'

Aleppo is looking deadly serious and Berenguela is about to gasp. 'Look, little girl, one needs to be married in order to have a husband. You are just a child and have not yet reached the marriageable age. Please stop with this fantasy, Aleppo.'

Now Aleppo turns back and says, 'My name is not Aleppo.' Berenguela puts her two palms either side of her head and sits down in disgust.

The little girl comes to sit next to her, caressing her back with her hands, saying, 'Look, Aunt Berenguela, I must find my husband and Ucles can really help me.'

'Aunt? How come you are calling me an aunt?' says a very surprised and extremely irritated Berenguela.

'You are not my aunt? What should I call you then?'

Aleppo is even more surprised than her.

Berenguela looks puzzled and says, 'Look, Aleppo, don't put pressure on me. I am Berenguela and you can call me Beren like the others do. But I am not your aunt. We are not a family. You must understand that.'

'What a strange thing you just have said. How can I call an elderly person by name!? My entire valley and beyond that valley, all of them are my aunts and uncles and cousins. No one has ever been so unkind to me before. Not even in Syria.'

She sounds so sad.

Berenguela looks at her and feels very unclear in her thoughts. Ucles comes close to them, some papers and a pen in his hands, and he asks Aleppo,

'Okay, Aleppo, what is your name?'

'Amal.'

'What is your surname?'

'What is a surname?'

'You don't know what a surname is?'

She shakes her head, negative.

'Well. A surname is the last part of one's name. Like my given name is Ucles. That is the place where my ancestors come from. And my surname is Cristofori. That is the name my family have been carrying for centuries, with pride.'

While he is talking to Aleppo, he gazes intensely at Berenguela's face. She seems to be deep in thought. Suddenly she turns to him and says, 'I thought you said that your name was 'de Seville'!'

It is Aleppo who cuts them short. She seems to have got the hang of the idea of something called a 'surname' and wants to contribute to the matter.

'Well, I come from the valley of Shangla, a beautiful place, not so far from the river Ghwarband, where the Pushtoon tribe of Isapzais live. You can make my surname 'Isapzai', just like your ancestral name.'

She looks at him expectantly. But with a shrewd smile on his face he continues. 'My dear Amal, that name 'Isapzai' was given to your clan by Alexander the Great in 330 BC, while passing through the Khyber Pass! Nowadays, they are simply called the Yousafzai. So, your first name is Amal and surname is Yousafzai. You are Amal Yousafzai. Just remember that for the future. You will always need your correct name. You understand that?'

Amal nods. Of course she understands.

'What is the name of your father?'

'Gaus.'

'Not only Gaus. He is called Gaus Yousafzai. And your mother's name is?'

'Ayesha Yousafzai.'

She now knows the system of names that she must always remember.

'Name of your husband?'

'Allah Shaheram. He belongs to another clan, Sherkhanzai of Utmanzi Charsadda.'

'Your date of birth?'

'Same day as the mule gave birth to a strong foal.'

'The date of your wedding?'

'When the moon was close to the earth, looking like a watermelon.'

'Your place of birth?'

'In the valley of Ghwarband.'

'Why did your husband leave you?'

'He did not.'

'What do you mean? How did you become separated?'

'I don't know. It was a long wedding day. Festivities took seven days. All the heads of the tribes came, along with their large families and distant kin. Tribes from Khyber Pakhtunkhwa, Rohilkhand, Tonk, Kohistan and the Mandan tribes. Tents were hoisted alongside the river Ghwarband.'

'Silk carpets were spread inside the tents and there were floral satin-covered bolsters in every corner of those, for the comfort of the guests. Lots of music was to be heard from a group of Sufi singers, who came from Alhambra. The best of the best cooks were hired from Lahore and the smell of the rich food spread through the air high above, so the shepherds too came down for the wedding feast.'

'Men were shooting blank bullets into the sky. I was decorated in my green and red satin wedding dress. My muslin veil was decorated with Indian pearls and gold. They said I was the most beautiful bride in the whole of the Pushtoon world! My mother gave me a glass of sweet drink and I dozed off on the white bed. After a while, an old woman from the other tribe came inside to pick up the white bed sheet. And suddenly she became furious and she began spitting on me.'

'Then there was shouting and shooting outside. The noble tribal leaders were demanding answers from a young male, who sounded like my newly-wed husband. 'Who had done it?'

'He said he had done it. They checked his upper legs and found a knife cut from which he was still bleeding. The old Chief of Peshwar came into the tent to ask me who had done it.'

'I did not know what to say.'

'Then my mother came to ask me the same question, 'who had touched me?' Everybody had touched me in that valley. What is wrong with touching? But my husband said it was he who had 'touched' me. I said my husband did not touch me. Because he was from the other side of the valley and I had never seen him before my marriage. Still he said he did. They wanted to punish us both. His uncles put us on horseback, tearing us away from our known world and that evening, while the group was resting next to the night fire and falling asleep, they whisked me away!'

'Then I was found in a hut on top of the mountain called Gunung Kemukus in Indonesia. That is the sex mountain, Mount Kemukus, where tourists come for free sex, which is a holy act, to reserve a seat in heaven. Every tourist, whether man or woman, must have sex with at least two strangers. That is a religious act. If one can have sex with two virgins, then one goes directly to heaven. Many guests came to visit me. Then there was one who bought me and sold me again to someone else.'

'He did not keep me either, because he wanted to have a virgin. Every time I was sold under the pretence that I was an untouched one. But they always asked me, how many men? How many? And how many? In that way I was sold to an old militant leader for ten dollars. But he also wanted to know, 'How many?'! There were always loads of sweet drinks and after waking up, my whole body ached. I cried for my mother to help me! I cried for my eldest sister. But by then, I was taken far and far away from them.'

The outside yard is feeling chilly now and they all shiver.

Possette comes out of the house to take Aleppo into her arms and holds her to her chest. She kisses her fondly and comforts her.

'Dear child, it is all over now. It will never happen again. You are free now. No one will ever come near you. You don't have to trust me, Aleppo. I could not save you then from all those dirty hands. Visigoth's beasts devoured you and I could do nothing but watch. But now things have changed. The Chief will save you. You can trust him, Aleppo.'

The little angel sobs and says, 'I have said many times, I am not Aleppo, but Amal. The media called me Aleppo, because they have rescued me from the hands of the gang of fundamentalist militants, from a camp in Aleppo where they kept sex-slaves!'

Ucles has a devilish smile on his face and asks, 'So! You are that Aleppo? What was the name of that guy who–'

Now Posette shouts at him, 'I think you must leave right now, before I call the police.'

'You want to call the police? Go ahead. And what will you tell the police about yourself? The law of the clergy and the law of a state are not the same. Are you sure you know that?'

He laughs at them like someone winning a game by cheating.

In the meantime, Simon has arrived, carrying a large spade in his hand. The maid follows him, gripping a large broomstick. He goes to the media guy and says, 'Look you, Hercules, go back to where you came from. I wouldn't mind going to jail for saving the honour of the ladies of my home.'

Simon looks aggressive now, as he is pushing Ucles with his spade.

He has a crazy smile on his face as he pushes Ucles and points at the dunes. The last thing that is audible from his mouth is that, 'Hey, any idea, how many could be resting under those sand dunes? Want to be one of them? No? You don't. So forget you have ever been here and avoid me.' The maid has a large smile on her plain, broad face as she says, 'And remember me too. 'Aaf', that is me, Aaf, who has lived here all her life.'

Only Aleppo is moaning in the arms of Posette. 'Please Posette, please stop Ucles. I have to find my husband. It was not my virgin marital blood that stained the white bed sheet, but his. He saved my family's honour by cutting his own body and staining the white bedsheet by his own blood. He wanted to prove my innocence. But he got caught. He was the only one who did not ask me, 'How many?'!'

'The film is not done and the show must go on!'

11

Tempus Fugit

Yes, time flies. Certainly for those who have not got much time on their hands. Those who are watching the clock and getting scared every time it chimes. They want to stop time for a while, so that they can do a bit more for themselves. But they can't stop the clock. The grandfather clock, which is standing downstairs in the farmhouse, is dutifully marking every second of time's progress.

Today is exactly the tenth of the month and tenth of the days, after the wedding of Posette and Ivan.

Upstairs, there is pin-drop silence. The two rooms next to each other are going through the struggle of time. In one room, a clergyman is sitting on a low stool next to Ivan's new double bed. His face is as expressionless as his black cloak. He is holding the holy book in both his hands, gazing at it through his thin gold-rimmed specs.

Probably he is reading some passages of it in his mind. Every now and then, the holy clergyman looks at Ivan's face. His thin-haired head is resting on a white pillow and his whole body is covered by a white quilt. On its greenish cover smiling dolphins are swimming in a clear lazuli-blue sea.

In the other room, Aaf and Berenguela are sitting next to Posette, who is lying on the floor, on top of an old mattress, covered with a white sheet. She is sweating and thirsty. Her face is pale and her body is showing signs of malnutrition. Her two arms are folded on her chest as if she is in some sort of prayer. Extreme fatigue is keeping her numb. Simon is walking like a polar bear outside the two rooms, not knowing what to do. It is all so oddly quiet. Only the grave tick-tock sound of the grandfather clock is audible, as if the clock is lamenting for not having enough time on its hands.

Suddenly Posette produces a strange whining cry, saying, 'Ivan, wait, please wait a bit longer–' and she moans with a loud heart-touching lament, as if she is searching for some divine help to deliver her from this life's sufferings. The baby pops out but it does not cry. Aaf is quick to cut the umbilical cord and ties it with a plastic clip. Berenguela snatches the baby to bring it into the other room. She sounds desperate, 'Look, Ivan. Look at your son'. Ivan smiles and closes his eyes.

At that very moment, the baby produces a loud cry and starts to shiver. Aaf comes running with some baby blankets and wraps it quickly. Berenguela is holding the baby to her chest and shushing it softly, 'Cry, little Ivan. Cry loud and hard. Let them know that you have returned to me! This Beren will take care of you. Even a fly would never dare to roam in the same air that you will breathe! I promise you that, my dear little Ivan. This time we'll make it. There will be no mistakes. There will be only you and me. Nobody else but just the two of us!'

The clergyman gets up.

'Well Berenguela, all is arranged about the final destination. We must not waste time unnecessarily. Shall we call the doctor for the death certificate?'

Berenguela nods.

'Yes, Father. Please do.'

Little Ivan cries for his mother's milk and Aaf takes him back to his mother, who is that Polish girl

Posette. Baby Ivan is in his mother's arms for the first time. He is sucking his mother's soft nipples and learning very fast how to survive outside his mother's womb.

Tears are rolling from Aaf's eyes. Are those the tears for losing her old master, with whom she grew up, hoping one day he would recognise her affections for him? Or are those tears of joy, that the impossible can happen? Or that her ill master has left an incredible gift for all of them as he did every Christmas, secretly, in that farmhouse?

The old doctor comes and writes two documents, one birth and one death certificate for two Ivans. The dead Ivan wanted to be buried next to his pal and long-time partner Jacques, in his back yard, among the wild rose bushes. Jacques had passed away in hospital a couple of years ago, when a strange disease called Aids was still not widely spoken about, and when it became known, only made everyone scared.

Jacques had wanted to rest with the others who are buried in the church yard. But that did not happen. He was a God-fearing person. But perhaps he was just only a God-fearing person, who did not know how to love God after all. Ivan wanted to avoid the fuss. They have been keeping a nice flower garden behind the farmhouse, where Jacques used to enjoy sunbathing and resting with a mug of dark, fair-trade coffee with Gouda cheese cubes. Now he is resting there forever. And so will the late Ivan.

A few people attended the funeral. Posette was looking at them, sitting on an old cane chair, from her window. Baby Ivan was attending his father's funeral, asleep on the chest of Berenguela, his aunt. Once more, the small funeral group looked at the baby, probably wanting to say some words of comfort.

Instead they saw the face of the deceased Ivan, smiling at them while sleeping in his wrapper. They looked at each other, making an ambiguous gesture. The unusual serenity of the whole event perhaps made them feel uncomfortable, and they left in dead silence, carrying a sense of oddness with them.

The priest came into the house to perform another holy act. Simon and Aaf were standing in the sitting room, next to each other in their Sunday clothes and the holy man pronounced them husband and wife. There was no one to raise his or her hand to claim any objection to this holy union and the newlywed couple did not seem to feel any pressure about being married.

After the holy event, they all drank tea with home-baked strawberry and cashew nut cakes. And the holy clergyman got a bottle of Irish whisky from the newly wedded couple for all the bother that he had to endure and they all wished him a good day and a very quiet evening afterwards.

Then they go to their own work. Simon has to take care of the barn. Berenguela keeps little Ivan on her chest, except when he has to be fed. Aaf takes care of the household. Everyone seems to have found a place of their own in that farmhouse. Except the other two, who remain outsiders.

Aleppo is sitting next to Posette, who is lying now on that old mattress, which is still spread on the floor. A grey sheet is covering her thin body from her neck to her toes. The little girl is rubbing her feet and sounding rather downhearted.

'Posette, they are a family now. Little Ivan even has an aunt. And you are his mother. I wish Berenguela could also be my aunt too. Or, perhaps, you could be my elder sister. Or at least something like a family of some sorts!'

Posette has a mournful smile on her face and she pulls Aleppo up onto her empty chest.

'Dear child, you have a family. Believe me, the Chief is your family. He'll sure come one day to fetch you and he'll take care of you. Trust me, little Aleppo. That time will come. Sure, I know, he will make things safe for you! It is just time, my dear child, a bit of time, that he needs.'

Aleppo pulls back and seems hurt as she says, 'Please, don't call me Aleppo. That was the name given by that media guy, who also abused me! My name is Amal.'

Posette sounds rather thoughtful as she says, 'Perhaps you should have a new name. Those old names are smeared with horrific memories. Perhaps we'll call you 'Lara'. Yes, from now one, you will be Lara. That is much better. You see, my dear, sometimes we have to hide ourselves behind our names.'

'Lara is a good name. Then how about my surname? The Yousafzai bit?' Could I call myself Lara Yousafzai?'

Aleppo wants to sound smart.

'No! I'm not so sure about that. Perhaps that name is not so safe for you to use. But you could ask the Chief about it.' Posette seems so distant now.

'Okay. I don't mind being a Lara since you like it too. I'll tell all of them that from now on, I am just Lara.'

Aleppo sounds enthusiastic.

'Yes. You must let them know that your real name is actually Lara. And you should ask Aaf to get some European clothes for you, like jeans and sweaters. No more walking in bare feet. You need simple and regular kids' shoes. Perhaps also a cap, to hide your face, when you go out. The church has a collection of old things for people who are in need. And don't walk too much outside, until the Chief comes and makes some arrangements for you.'

Before Posette can stop, Aleppo laughs at her with an adult's mockery and says, 'Posette, you are out of your mind. How can the Chief do anything for me? He has not got a house of his own? He got no job, no money, not even his own mother to cry about! Nothing at all! He lives on stale bread and cold tap water. He does not even have a toilet? Remember? How can he ever help anyone?'

She is now looking directly into Posette's eyes, as if she needs a confirmation of her statements.

Posette closes her eyes to open her mind. She tries to recall the night that she had to spend in his one-room apartment. That room had nothing comforting. Yet it was full with joy and happiness. She had had the happiest moment of her life in that tiny space, on that top floor. Suddenly her heart longs for that place. Her mind desires to be there once more and to sit on his dirty sofa-bed. And drink cold water from his tap in a used paper cup.

Posette looks at Aleppo and lets out a deep sigh.

'Lara, you are still a child. You don't know who has got what and who has not. Would you be happy if he was a person who has everything and is nasty? Or would you rather want to see him as a kind and caring person who has nothing?'

Aleppo nods her head vehemently and says, 'It is better to have everything. Certainly a place of your own. Then nobody can throw you out on the streets. You are not upset in your own house and you can always keep your doors shut against unwanted thugs. But how come you don't have a house of your own, Posette?'

Posette looks at Aleppo's expectant eyes and wants to be honest with the little girl. 'I have tried to buy a little place of my own. But I could not get a mortgage from the bank, because I did not have a permanent job.'

'But you had loads of money and you had a job with Visigoth?'

Now Posette laughs.

'Lara, that job is not considered a regular job. A job involves a monthly salary, which is deposited in the bank account of the employee every month. And I did not have loads of money to buy a place of my own. I had to pay a lot of bills for the others. But you cannot be expected to understand that.'

Aleppo nods her head and says, 'Perhaps not. But why didn't you tell me about this mortgage businesses before? That dirty old bank director who comes for me? He pays such loads of cash to Visigoth! And that disgusting solicitor guy, with his innocent baby face! Often they come together and they fight over me? I could have asked them to arrange a mortgage for you. Then you could buy a small apartment. A two-room place, so you and me could share one and the Chief could have the other one? And your place could have been a 'home' for all of us! Shall I go back to Visigoth and ask him for those two dirty ones to come? I am sure I could arrange that.'

Posette sits up straight now with fright.

'No. No, Lara. You must not go near to Visigoth anymore. You see, his job was to keep you safe, until your family arrives. But he also got greedy like the others. The old white guys have fallen for you like those in other countries.'

Aleppo seems happy to know that her family is searching for her and clasps her hands in joy.

'My family is searching for me? I could go home? I could see my mother and sisters again?'

'No! No, dear Lara. What I have heard by eavesdropping on the conversations which Visigoth was having with a couple of strange guys is that your family is trying to trace you only to save their family honour. You have destroyed the honour of your family and your family must avenge it by killing you! That's why we have to change your name and your clothes. You must take a new identity. And the Chief must help you. Because there is no-one else out there for us but him. Do you understand the ugliness of the situation around us, Lara?'

Aleppo shivers as she recalls the many honour killings around her valleys. It is not just one bullet. A bullet is far too valuable for an unchaste girl.

There is no escape for such a sinner. She will always be found and will be tied up on a bed. And there will be many male visitors in her room, till to the end of her last bit of breathing. Then her body will be set on fire, dust to dust and ashes to ashes, so that others can watch and learn their own lessons from it.

The one important lesson which is taught to every female child right from their birth is, 'Keep your chastity safe. Until a married husband is there to prove that you are still a virgin, so that your male guardians can kiss you with pride and your husband can receive gifts from his own family for finding a real virgin for his family.' It is all a matter of honour for both of the families. Its clean history will be written down for chastity's sake.

No. She does not want to be killed for something she is not guilty of. She has committed no sin. She did not take her chastity away by herself. Someone must have done it for her! Someone inside her family? Someone she trusted and who was close to her. No. She will not die for a crime which has been committed by somebody else. She can't recall anything. But some dirty guy had taken advantage of her innocence, although she's no closer to knowing the truth.

There were too many drinks to enjoy, prepared from poppy seeds. During the warm summer evenings, when a gentle breeze is touching people's skins with love and tenderness on the top of the mountains, and when all ladies have fallen asleep on the charpoys, which were laid on the green grass, while no one had any sense of what was going on around them. When babies did not even cry for their mother's milk. Where were those thugs hanging around then, who were busy stealing the innocence of little girls? Who were they? No, she must not give up. She will continue living, with another name, taking another disguise. From now on, she is just 'Lara'. She is just Lara, without the surname Yousafzai.

'The film is not done and the show must go on!'

12

De Profundis

There is a polite knock on the door and Aaf comes in with the baby. This strange baby hardly ever cries, as if he is never hungry or never in any sort of discomfort. Yet, he has to be fed on time. Posette looks at her baby and immediately closes her nostrils. A pungent stink hurts her sense of smell. The stench knocks on some events out of her distant memories. This malodour is known to her. Exactly the same awful reek she has experienced before.

Probably it was in a small village, where she had been working as a new doctor. A middle-aged looking guy would come with a strange sort of complaint. His body would stink like a beast from hell and no one could stand near him. Even the air around him was wrapped with an offensive stench. He wanted to be cured so that he could get married. His mother had chosen a girl from the nearby village. But the rumours had reached that family too concerning his unusual illness. His future wife refused him on the grounds that she would not be able to live with a husband stinking like a hellish beast.

That guy wanted her to help him. He wanted to sit next to her and talk about his physical problems. He said that he was in his mid-thirties then. A rather well built fellow. He sat down next to her and she threw up in front of the other patients, who were sitting on the bench which was fixed to the floor. They laughed at her and she ran away from her practice. She had cursed herself for being a physician often enough. But this time it was unbearable. After that incident, she did not dare to face any of the villagers and she just had to leave.

After that ugly event, the guy never came back to her. Later on she heard that his body had been found in the nearby river. Someone had advised him to go to India to take baths regularly in the holy river Ganges, which might carry away the bugs that he had been carrying on his body. There are so many Hindu gods and the Ganges is one of them. One of the gods might bestow mercy upon him. And if a Hindu god could not cure him, who else on this globe could perform such a miracle?

But as he did not know how to reach the river Ganges, or even how to reach India itself, instead, he had chosen a river which was close to his own homestead. What else could it have been? Apparently he never used any drugs. She had thought about that patient for many years. She did not know what could cause a human body to stink in such a horrific manner! Did she ever feel guilty subconsciously concerning her patient's death?

She gets back to her present situation only to find that tears are welling up in her eyes and flowing down her cheeks. She whispers, 'I can't suckle him anymore! Take him back to Berenguela.'

Aaf takes the baby and turns away, while Posette is sobbing,

'Oh, Ivan. Why couldn't you stay with me a bit longer? Oh, my baby Ivan. I can't hold you in my arms anymore. Oh, my baby, why do you have to have that horrible stink?'

Lara comes near to comfort her and says, 'I don't smell anything odd about baby Ivan! You must be imagining things, Posette? Babies do not stink?'

'No. Normally babies do not stink. They smell like babies usually do. But this baby does. Because he is not a normal baby! Don't you think so too, Lara?'

Lara tries to think and says, 'Of course he is a normal baby. Ivan was his daddy and you are his mom. So what else does he need to be normal?'

Posette has not got a reasonable answer for this heavyweight question. All she knows is that something is not quite right about the whole thing, what has been happening during the last ten months and afterwards.

After she had spent one night in that one-room apartment on the top floor, her life had changed, for the better or for the worse, that she can't see. A horrible fear creeps into her heart. She tries to find solace of some kind. Her life has never been a quiet one. She has experienced the worst of the worst. What more can happen to her? An unknown fear shakes her up again.

Baby Ivan is now hanging from the neck of his aunt Berenguela, from a thick piece of strong Mexican zigzag cloth. His milk bottles are kept ready by Aaf. He sleeps on the chest of Berenguela, who sleeps in the corner room downstairs. Only

Posette and Lara live upstairs, in Posette's room. They comfort each other and talk about nothing sensible. Sometimes Lara goes downstairs and tries to get herself involved with the farm work. But both Simon and Aaf seem reluctant to have her around, although they say nothing.

One day, Simon comes upstairs to talk to Posette. He takes his old hat off his head and hesitates a long while. After enquiring about her health, he tells her in some dismay that some strangers have been seen, sneaking around the farm, who are not European! They come as quietly as foxes and disappear like evil spirits in the dunes. It is rather eerie. Anything Posette could suggest about this? Should they call the police, if that would be useful?'

Posette shivers inside her chest but reacts lightly and says, 'No, Simon. We mustn't waste the police's time for no valid reason. You are just imagining things. They must be refugees from some Middle Eastern countries, looking for fun in the sand dunes. We have such a lot of them nowadays. Never mind them. But perhaps Aaf could go to the church one day and fetch some clothes for our little Lara. Some European clothes would fit her nicely.'

Simon looks surprised and looking at both of

them says, 'Lara!'

'Yes. Lara. That is my real name, Simon. And Posette is actually my cousin, you know? We are not strangers.'

Simon now looks even more puzzled.

'Okay, love. So I'll tell Aaf that she must collect some clothes for Lara. And not for Aleppo.'

'Yes, Simon, exactly. And we don't know any Aleppo or Amal. I am Charlemagne of Granada and this is my cousin Lara. We are a family now. And if anyone might get curious about us, tell them that I am going through a very rough time, losing my husband and at the same time having a baby. My cousin has come to take care of me, since other family members are not available right now.'

Simon nods his head acceptingly and says, 'I got it, missus. But I think from now on, Aleppo, I mean Lara, better keeps herself inside the house, next to you. I mean, you need help. You are depressed and you need someone around you all the time. Aaf and me are doing okay. The farm does not need any help right now. And Marco is willing to come here for a few days. That is, if you want. It is getting cold on the streets and he is getting tired of the wandering life. So he is willing to enjoy a domestic life for a while and milk the cows. Isodore has sent a message that as soon as the Chief has found some decent clothes for Marco, he'll be here. You see, Marco only likes suits and black shiny shoes. But you may decide. You are the boss now.'

Posette looks surprised and says, 'But how about Berenguela? She should make decisions for all of you?'

'No. She is busy with the baby and she is not to be disturbed. Little Ivan inherits everything and until he is eighteen, you may decide for all of us.'

Simon looks at her respectfully and says, 'Aaf said women feel down after having a baby. Her own mother could not stand her around either. So she was given away. Of course she does not know her birth mother. But she loves her mom every second of her life. So will little Ivan. And you are around. You are not going away?'

There is a trill in his voice, as if he is expecting the worst. What might happen, if things change at the farm? How would their lives be without this little farmhouse? And that street vagabond Marco, who had always searched for a home, who is coming here with the heartfelt hope of finding a place among friends? No one should ever try to erase the hope of others. Besides, there is enough room at the farm, which can offer an honest shelter for a good soul. Above all, she is the boss now and she has the power to be a boon to those who are around her.

Posette feels cold with fear. There might be something frightful going on? She has had no news from the city of Amsterdam for many months now. She was driven to a very different world by a strange power. But Isodore is there. Berenguela has gone there regularly? And of course the Chief is still there. If anything frightening is going on, then they must let her know! Why is Isodore sending Marco here? He is a street vagabond, who has no human bonds. How can he help them? But on the other hand, no-one really knows anything about that Marco guy.

Who are those guys who are looking at the house like foxes, as Simon claimed? She feels cold horror in her mind. She was married to a very ill guy, who was an HIV patient and who is dead now. She has a baby with him, the baby which stinks so horribly that she can't hold it in her arms, although she is its biological mother. She is not suckling her own baby! The baby has a right by birth to be able to suck his mother's milk and she is denying that to him! She is letting her own child down. Her baby is living from a milk-bottle.

And no one says anything, as if it is all normal, like sunrise and sunset. Every time she looks at the baby, she sees old Ivan smiling at her. That baby is a second drop of water of his own father's image. She feels rather dizzy now as she says, 'Okay, let Marco come. We need helping hands here after all.'

She has only one question on her subdued mind. Where is he? She has not seen him after her wedding. Doesn't he know that she has got a baby now? Of course he does. But he hasn't come to see it! It hurts her feelings. How could he not come to see her baby? She feels really upset now. Lara has been witnessing all of it and she says thoughtfully, 'Don't worry about the Chief, Posette. He is with Isodore now. Helping him in the bicycle repair shop. I have been sending him food regularly. He is not hungry anymore.'

'You have been sending him food? How?'

Her eyes are wide open now, full of surprise and something like fear.

'Through a driver. I wait for him at the corner of the hedgy path and he knows that I am waiting for him. But from now on, perhaps I rather not wait for him anymore. Maybe Aaf can do that.'

Posette holds this graceful child in her arms and kisses her intensely as she says, 'Oh dear child, thank you. Thank you. I have been so worried about him. Only I was too busy to mention it.' She feels so grateful to this vivacious child. She feels that she must protect her by all possible means from the cruel world that awaits outside. She must think hard and find a way to rescue her.

She gets up and looks outside through the window. There are two very tall guys at the gate, talking with Simon. He is shaking his head in such a manner as if a poisonous insect is sitting on top of his nose.

She looks at the two guys and feels a wave of fear passing through her body. Those guys are not just regular tourists or so. They are tall and their heads and faces are covered with some kind of masks. Their clothes are new, as if they just have bought them. They look as if they have never worn these sorts of clothes in their earlier lives. They are looking at the house and their eyes are searching for something, like watchful and trained eagles.

One thing is very clear about them. They are

not pretending to be something they are not. They are not tourists for sure. Lara comes to stand near Posette but she quickly pushes her down and says, 'Keep yourself down and don't come near the window.'

Lara can sense fear in her throat and her heart is beating furiously. She briefly recalls the experiences which Amal had to go through and, afterwards, Aleppo of Syria. She is sitting on the floor now and shaking her head. No! No! She is not Amal and she is not Aleppo. She is Lara now and no one will ever harm her anymore. She will survive. They have to contact the Chief.

That homeless guy can't do anything useful to help himself. But in a very strange way, he can always help others. He has no food for himself. Yet he collects food for others. Of course Posette was right about him. She just has to find him to ask for a hiding place for her, as a stopgap.

While she is thinking all of this, Posette sees an old orange van approaching through the serpentine paths of the sand dunes. The van passes the two guys who were talking with Simon and comes to a stop just in front of the gate. A guy in a grey suit steps out, a bit awkwardly, and looks around with serenity. Now Aaf has come out of the house and hands a plastic shopping bag to the van driver. The driver gets into his van and heads for the hedgy path again. The two strangers are not visible now.

The suited guy is greeted by Simon and they chat about something. Posette feels the need to stand up again and take back control into her hands. It seems as if she has been away from her life for aeon after aeon. And now it is time for her to collect all of it. She looks at Lara and says, 'Those two are gone now and a new one has arrived. That could be Marco. Please help me to the bath and let's have some clean clothes now.' Lara smiles at her and stretches out her thin elegant arm towards her and says with a pretty smile, 'Hold my arms, cousin Posette. You should have the prettiest dress today.'

So they go down and Posette has a bath in her white bathroom and there is a pink floral dress waiting for her, the dress Ivan had ordered from a catalogue book. They were planning to christen their baby in that dress. There was also baby clothing and a shirt for Ivan too. Now Ivan is gone and she is left alone. What is her task now? Berenguela has taken the baby, which is hanging from her neck twenty-four hours a day. Simon and

Aaf are taking care of the farm. What can she do as Ivan's widow?

She gets out of the bath and goes directly into the kitchen, where all of them are already sitting as if waiting for her. They all look very thoughtful and are waiting for her to say something. Marco stands up only to introduce himself as 'Marco' and then sits down again. Lara comes near her in her black leggings and red T-jama. They all stare at her and Posette looks at Aaf and says, 'We need some boys clothes for Lara and a boy's name perhaps. Her hair must be cut very short immediately.'

Lara shakes her head vehemently, saying she loves combing her long hair and she will never be parted from it. Her own mother would be very upset, if she did something as naughty as that.

Simon looks at Aaf and they both seem puzzled. Only Marco looks at Posette and coughs. 'Ma'am, forgive me saying so. But that is not the safest way to disguise a person.'

Posette looks at him questioningly. 'What do you mean? Do you know what is going on here? Any idea of the amount of danger that we are in?'

'Yes. I have heard it all and I could guess it too. You see, ma'am, I have been on the streets for many years. But before that I had a different sort of life. Some may even call it a decent life. I have understood that two guys are searching for a little girl whose name is Aleppo. And a very angry Simon replied to them that no Aleppo is living here. Not even an Amal! So they had their answers. They know that Amal or Aleppo is here.'

Posette looks at Simon as if she wants to say, 'Oh Simon! What have you done?'

She sees Simon's guilty face and turns back to Marco, who says, 'Look, ma'am, the most obvious way to disguise her would be dressing her up as a boy. But that is common practice and those thugs know it too. We have to bring her to a safe place.'

'And where will that safe place be?'

But Lara interrupts Posette and says, 'Please, call the Chief. I can live in his place, can't I?'

Posette shakes her head.

'But that would be sending the chick into the custody of a fox. Don't you know who his neighbour is?'

'That is exactly what we are going to do. The safest place to hide from a cheetah is the Lion's Den itself.'

They all are now looking at this girl from an

unknown valley of the Pak-Afghan border, of which they have no idea at all. They seem puzzled and frightened by her looks.

An amulet of lapis lazuli is hanging from her beautifully curved marble-like neck, from a piece of purple silk thread. That fairy child looks at them, opening wide her emerald green eyes and says reassuringly, 'Let's find the Chief!'

'The film is not done and the show must go on!'

13

The Serpentine Path

The Chief is running down from his top floor one-room apartment in a hurry. There are so many reasons for him to run. He must open the door of the bicycle repair shop before the new boys get there. They are boys sent there by the vocational schools, where under-aged foreign children go in order to learn how to work with their inexperienced hands, so that when they are back in their own homeland, they will be able to use the skills they have acquired in a great European country, which has sheltered them in the first place.

On the other hand, it is the best way to keep them busy, so that they will not have the chance to mess up themselves. So they are sent to school to learn European skills and the Western way of life, a way of life that they may have some knowledge about. But they must not adopt it for themselves.

It is a government project and it is Isodore's task to teach them all about bikes. They are refugee children, who are without their parents and are seeking asylum in the Netherlands. These boys are at a difficult age, between teenage and adult, which means that they are neither elderly young boys, nor young adults. They are sort of hanging in between boyhood and manhood so to speak and they don't know exactly who they are, and they don't care much about bicycles either. But they come here because they are told to by the authorities. And of course the main attraction is the girls hanging around the bicycle repair shop. And the girls like to flirt with them too. Araaagh! Oh, yeah, they do.

It works both ways. For many white girls, it used to be fashionable to go out with foreign guys. Walking home from a pub in the middle of the night with a tall and large, strong black guy would give them a sense of security. Having a relationship with a brown South Asian guy would give them a cosmopolitan look. Sometimes they would even get married and, if they were lucky, they would even live together, till their second child was born. But eventually, they would move back to their own culture.

The young white lady in question would be a middle-aged lady by then and she would find comfort with a white guy after all. And the foreign guy would find a partner among friends of his own culture. That too is a matter of comfort. But nowadays, these sorts of mixed relationships are not so common and the minds of young girls are changing. They would rather hang around with people of a similar colour and that gives lots of comfort in their homes as well. But these refugee boys don't know that. They live in the camps for asylum seekers and their movements are monitored for their own good.

But that is all about political set-up and no-one needs to be bothered by it. He is here for Isodore, who is ill. His back is giving him trouble and he sounds rather down. His cheerfulness is gone. His mental ability to do things is below zero. And that is probably all because Berenguela is not here. She is not coming anymore to sit in his bicycle repair shop and she does not bring freshly made bread and jam either. Instead a van driver is bringing it for them. Suddenly the Chief feels immensely guilty. That driver has been carrying food for him and he has never ever even thanked him and has never even asked his name! How ungrateful of him!

He jumps from the last step of his house and feels he needs to go to the toilet most urgently. It is morning and the streets are already rather crowded. He cannot just go behind a tree next to the canal. He looks around intently thinking of going to the pub and asking them politely for the use of their toilet. Those people should know that he can't really spend fifty cents for using their toilet facilities.

He feels rather unhappy that they live in such a city, where money flies in the air and the government is earning money from the air too, yet people like the Chief and tourists have to pay more than fifty cents for an emergency reason like using the toilets. It feels so inhuman.

In other decent countries, like England for example, the use of public-toilets is completely free. Chain shops and supermarkets offer free toilet use. Big individual shops too. Even the fast food shops like McDonald's offer free toilet and baby care areas. But the same fast food shops are earning lots of money here in the Netherlands by collecting coins from the pockets of the public.

Someone should protest about this inhuman practice of robbing. Perhaps there will come a day when someone will discuss this subject with the Dutch queen if possible.

He has been just searching for the possibility of what to do when suddenly a tall coarse figure approaches him and says, guffawing, 'Need to use a toilet, Chief?'

Now he looks at him and his eyebrows shrink. Without looking at him, he follows and they enter into his basement's beauty shop. Visigoth shows the way to the toilet by a gesture of his finger. He has never seen a toilet like this in his entire life. The whole place is covered with wall-to-wall mirrors and shines like a glass house. White towels are rolled up on the shelves, next to perfume bottles. He does not know where he is.

He comes out and Visigoth and another guy follow him. That is the apish guy, whose face is now covered with a thick, dark beard. They are now walking next to him. He stops and looks at them with irritation.

'So, Chief, how were my toilets? Are you feeling comfortable now? You see, Chief, I made it all for her. I created everything according to her taste. She has been the artist behind my business. But now it is not the same. You see, without her, this place is not vibrant anymore!'

Visigoth has a low spirited voice now and the Chief feels rather awkward that this sycophantic guy still does not mention a thing about Aleppo! What is the matter with this guy? Where does the mystery lie?

In the meantime the other guy comes forward and kneels down in front of him on the street, so that he can no longer move forward. His two palms are folded into each other as if he is praying to the divinity for a precious gift and he says, 'Look, Chief, you don't know me. But I do know you from her. She had a great respect for you. Please send her a message for me saying that Dalir Baghatur-i can't work without her advice. My job is finished. I am ruined.'

He is sobbing now like a child. But Visigoth goes back to his old temperament and howls at him, 'Look, Chief, you dirty little Indian from Arizona, look what she has done to this guy. I mean this guy is a psychologist and he can't help his patients without discussing their business with her! Can you imagine such a successful professional guy's job is depending on a whore like that, who is a hell of a slut, and also a doctor and a very good one at that. She has treated the whole of the red-light district and has done a hell of a job. Araagh, where did you hide her?'

Suddenly Visigoth stops his angry rant but the apish guy, Dalir, remains sitting on the ground, sobbing. The Chief looks behind him and sees that remarkable unique wheelchair moving towards them. The frightening movement of that particular chair makes every heart shatter with fear. Now he realises the alertness of Visigoth and lets go a relaxed sigh. And he says to himself, 'Just in time, Demi Monde.'

The wheelchair stops in front of them and the majestic lady sitting in it looks at all of them with her sharp eyes, full of mascara and dark Sudanese collyrium. Her made-up face can't hide the fact that once upon a time she must have been a rare beauty. But there is something about her skin. Most of her body is always covered by very expensive clothes. The small visible parts do not reveal much about her true colour.

The Chief always feels a sort of numbness seeing her and never really knows how to greet her. It is her graceful personality and her majestic presence that cause such a heart-throbbing effect. The wheelchair comes to a halt near them and the guy who has been pushing it moves back a bit further, as if she wants him to be out of earshot.

'Now, Chief, don't you know how to say 'hallo' to ladies?'

Is Lucretia serious with this question? He mumbles something in his mouth.

But the lady doesn't need any answer from him as she continues towards the tall guy and says, 'And now, Visigoth, do you use the toilets at night?'

'Yes, madam. Yes, of course. I have got very beautiful and clean toilets in my business.'

'Obviously you have. Part of your business, hey? From now on, I want every apartment to have a toilet and warm water. You think you can arrange that in one day's time?'

There is an air of very cold and severe disdain in Lucretia's voice and Visigoth is showing signs of discomfort as if his bladder is causing him trouble.

'Yes, I can, Madam. Of course I can. Got a friend from Bulgaria, who is an expert in making bathrooms and toilets. You see, madam, he is a well-known biologist in his own country. But also very good at making toilets. Now he works for a Russian building company here in Amsterdam and is earning enough to go back to his family soon. I will contact him right away. Sorry. Forgive me, madam. I need to use the toilet now.' Visigoth is not visible anymore and the psychologist Dalir has started to follow him slowly.

Soon they are both gone and the lady looks upon him.

'And now, Chief, rumour goes that your life is not safe anymore? How is life actually?'

He keeps his head bent down as he answers, 'Life is still three-fold and still in three different colours. The past is dark. The present is not a rainbow. And the future is white. Yes, you are right. I need a chest to hide a precious gem from a far-away star and can't trust anyone!'

Now she seems to be smiling and she looks up at him fully. 'Always talking wisely like your grandfather, hey? But he was wrong and you are also wrong. Trust is one thing you must always have, even in a most poisonous serpent. Hearts of all sorts, whether they are animal or human, become cold from NOT trusting others. Bring that little gem of yours to my place. You know where I live, don't you?'

'Did I say that 'it' was little?'

He feels scared now.

'Watch your words, Chief. You are much more mindless than that grandfather of yours! What a pity.'

Lucretia lets go a deep sigh. The guy in the shiny black clothes reappears like a ghost and starts to push the wheelchair. The queen of the red-light district is sitting on her wheelchair as if the Mughal empress Mumtaz Mahal is sitting on the Takht-e-Taus, the peacock throne built by the Mughal emperor Shah Jahan.

That world-famous jewelled throne couldn't be more impressive than her unique wheelchair, which makes everyone alert and shaky. He shivers with fear. That lady knows every single detail of this city and of the universe. How does she collects all that news and from whom? At the same time, he feels less burdened. After all, he can certainly trust this lady with his little gem. Lucretia must have a safe chest for it.

'The film is not done and the show must go on!'

14

Dies Irae

With a relieved and happy heart, he runs towards the bicycle repair shop. He realises that he has the keys of the shop and if Isodore should have come, he wouldn't be able to get in. From the corner of the street he can see that two boys are standing in front of the shop. They are laughing heartily with two young giggling girls.

These girls are tall white Dutch girls and he has told those boys not to meddle with them. It is not easy to be an asylum seeker and try to find human contact at the same time. Those girls will never understand the agony which these young boys are going through. He must warn them strongly and he will not let Isodore be easy on them. In these sorts of situations, things can only go wrong.

The two boys turn their back on seeing him

coming. The girls move away, giggling and laughing about themselves. He opens the huge wooden door and they go in. One of the boys goes to make coffee. The other one is searching for the cookie box. Not finding it on the table, he gets annoyed and asks the other boy, 'Now, Mongkut, where is the box?'

Mongkut mocks him with his limited Dutch and says, 'I don't have a sweet tooth like Syrians do. You are always looking for the box, Firas Hadad. Do they always eat cookies in the Hadad family?' Now Firas seems angry and says, 'Yes they do. They are not stingy Siamese people.'

Another boy comes rushing in and they all turn to him. Both Mongkut and Firas mock him.

'Look, Chief, the Portuguese prince has arrived. Shall we salute him for being so late?'

The boy has a large smile on his face and says, 'I, Breno Morales, am never late. This morning I had to go to hospital to give some blood. The laboratory nurse has taken much too much blood from me. My head got funny. I am feeling dizzy now. I need some sweet cookies.'

He looks around madly to find the cookie box, as if that box is the answer to life and death now.

Not seeing it he gets upset and shouts, 'I'll find that damn cookie box and I'll fill it up with big chunks of round chocolate cookies. And I'll not be stingy to my neighbours and I'll give them all a large chocolate cookie. Well, I'll do that someday.'

The box is visible under a pile of cardboard boxes but it is empty! Breno shouts and says, 'How come no-one has kept one cookie for me?' Firas laughs at him and says, 'How come you don't ask your mother? How come you are here with us, being Portuguese? We are asylum seekers and we have no place to hide. We get drowned in the sea and we get burned in our own country by the international political bombs. And we don't cry for a cookie!'

'Only a very stupid Portuguese street boy would cry for a cookie,' Mongkut adds his bit of mockery. But now they do not laugh at each other's jokes. Maybe their jokes have been so crude that it hurts everyone's feelings.

The Chief feels that this argument could turn into a nasty fight. Perhaps Firas has had bad news from the IND[1]. The Dutch immigration office

---

1 Immigratie en Naturalisatiedienst ('Immigration and Naturalisation Department').

is becoming stricter and stricter every day. The government's policy is to close the border and tell asylum seekers that it is a small country after all and maybe all foreigners could try to find a larger country, which might have more space and more air to breathe.

Breno shakes a fist at him and says, 'Look, Firas Hadad, I didn't send bombs to your country. Why don't you find the people responsible and ask them for damages for the problems they are causing to your homeland? They are responsible for helping you, not me?'

A van stops, making a horrible screeching sound with its tyres on the street. A beer-bellied man comes in with a large shopping bag in his hands and says, 'Sorry guys. Forgive me for being late. Aaf was not feeling very well and Posette had to make everything ready alone. Yeah, it all takes time.'

Then he looks at the new boy and introduces himself to him by shaking hands, 'Hey, me Henk. You know me, I am always in my van and never have the time to stretch my legs. And if I do, then I get such a cramp in the leg muscles. The pain is horrible. There is no-one to give a massage in the middle of the night. Sleeping in the van is no more fun either.'

He is now stretching his arms and legs in slow motion as if he is still sitting inside his van.

Mongkut looks at the middle aged man with huge sympathy and asks him, 'Are you also a refugee like us?'

'Why don't you ask COA for a room?'[2]

'Is your procedure finished? Have they thrown you out on the street?'

Three questions come from three asylum seeker boys and Henk looks puzzled.

He has no idea what COA is and what is meant by the word 'procedure'. But he nods his head.

'No, guys. I have not asked anyone for a room yet. But I will do so soon. You see, my legs have got crooked and curved from sleeping in the van. I'll ask Posette if I can sleep in her barn. There is lots of space there and Marco is planning to make a room next to Aaf and Simon's room. Of course I could share the room with Marco. But he snores too much.'

---

2   COA means: CENTRALE OPVANG ASIELZOEKERS ('Central Shelter for Asylum Seekers').

The three boys laugh their hearts out, although they do not understand everything Henk has said. He goes on, 'But the farm is getting in better shape now, since Posette has taken charge. She is the boss there now, as anyone will care to know. And the baby is growing like a green cabbage every day and looking like his father, the late Ivan, if you know what I mean.'

None of them are looking at the Chief. If they had, they could have seen that the mention of one particular name has made his face blue with misery. Her name is hurting him. At the same time, he is longing to hear her name. He wants to know if she is okay, being the boss of the farm. But he does not like to hear about her baby. That is too much for him.

Henk looks at the Chief and says, 'There is a message for you, Chief, from the boss, I mean the lady of the farm. That is, if you could keep something safe for her?'

He does not want to look at him. But he says, 'Tell your boss that it is all arranged and she can send it to me tomorrow morning very early, before daybreak.'

Henk seems happy to hear it.

'Okay. Missus will be happy. I'll bring her the news. Maybe she will come to bring it. But maybe not. She hasn't been out of her farm for many months now.'

His heart jumps. Is she really going to come? Will it be possible to see her again? How will it be seeing her after such a long time? Will she recall him at all? But perhaps she will not come. She is a different person now. Now she is the boss. She has the prestige and honour that she deserves. Still, it will be nice seeing her again. There is something, which belongs to him, that is gone with her. Something which has never returned to him. An immense sadness fills his chest. He feels suffocated and he feels that he can't bear to hear her name anymore.

He looks at the three boys, who resemble very much his own life. But yet, those boys have something that he does not. Those boys talk about their clear cut memories, which he does not have. His memories are vague and shadowy. Those boys talk about their families and some of their relatives have faced a brutal death.

But he has got no such memories. No-one has died. Yet no-one is alive either. He feels he can't be with these people, who have got all of it and he has got nothing. Jealousy makes him feel sick. He wants to get away from all of it. He looks at the van driver and says, 'Look, Henk, could you please come back here, say about half past four, to shut down this place and bring the key to me tomorrow morning?'

He does not wait for an answer. He leaves the bicycle repair shop in a hurry, as if the world is going mad in his absence. He runs towards the only place where he can be himself. He comes back to his room. He goes to lie down on his sofa and looks at the poster photo of his grandfather, the grand Chief of the Arizona Mountains. Today his heart gives up. He can't even complain to his next of kin. He looks at his grandfather's eyes and says, 'One day, when the day will come, I'll put you in a golden frame! Can you hear me? Can you wait that long?'

Probably his grandfather answers him. But he does not have the heart to hear him. He feels that his heart is actually a very tiny thing, which is only there to pump blood around for circulation throughout his body. It is a piece of mechanical machinery and it has no function in emotional commitments. He wishes he had a different kind of heart inside his chest.

A softer and kinder heart, which wouldn't be jealous of her! A loving and warm heart, which would always be full of blessings for her baby. But perhaps it is better not to feel anything at all about her. Yeah, that is just what he is going to do. He will just give up her memories too. He has got no-one and he deserves none.

He runs down to find the streets again. He looks like an erratic person. His mind is perplexed and he feels agitated. He feels the need to see some known faces. There were some kind faces on the street once. Like Marco and Simon and their acquaintances of the streets. Maybe he can find some of them and maybe he can share his life with them. The life of a tramp is not that difficult. You are a nobody and you don't need to care about yourself. Yes, he will just do that.

He walks through the streets and comes near the Central Station. It is rather cold and he feels chilly. His only dress has always been his yellow-brownish leather jacket from Arizona, given to him by his grandfather, the grand Chief of the Mountains.

He looks around and sees the apish guy, who is talking with a street woman. She is a Moroccan girl, who has been hanging around on the streets for many years now. No matter what, whether it is raining or snowing, she is always to be found there, in her very short dress under her thick black rubber coat. Once upon a time, she was the beauty of the streets. But now, excessive use of drugs has crashed her whole body.

But what is Dalir doing with her? He goes close to them and the woman looks at him and says, 'Chief, this guy is bothering me. Please ask him to give me some money. I need a shot. My body is aching. Please Chief, have mercy, please!'

He looks at the woman and realises that once he made a promise, swearing on the memory of his mother, that he would never use drugs and would never have anything to do with drugs. He looks at Dalir questioningly and he says, 'Believe me, Chief, I did not want anything from her. All I wanted is a piece of a message about her! Oh Chief, please help me. We all are going mad without her. Visigoth is going out of his mind. He is my patient now and even I can't help him. He can't sleep on his right side anymore!'

The Chief looks at him with narrowed eyes. And Dalir begins to explain, 'You see, Chief, all of the Visigoths from the beginning of the centuries, the first half of the night, they have slept on the right side of their body. And for the second half, they have slept on the left side, which is good for the heart. Or so they believe. Our Visigoth had no problem so far to keep continuing with his family's tradition. But now he can't be faithful to the family rituals. The first four hours work. But the next four hours do not.'

The street woman looks at Dalir and spits in his face. Then she turns and says, 'Go to hell with that bitch Posette.'

He looks around and shame creeps up on him. He feels enormous sympathy for this Dalir guy and looks at him without a shred of hatred.

'Dalir, let's walk to Isodore's bicycle shop. There are some nice young boys working there. Maybe you would like to have a cup of coffee with them. Oh, and they would very much like to have some freshly made chocolate cookies from V&D. You know, the ones where one side is chocolate and the other side is covered with crushed nuts of all sorts?'

What relief he feels in his chest. At the same time

shame also creeps in. How could he let down his friends Isodore and Berenguela? He has promised to help them. And now, he has left their shop in the care of some brainless young asylum seeker boys, who are always fighting with each other. How could he be so empty headed himself?

In the meantime, Dalir comes out of the bread department of the V&D, which used to be a chain of posh shops until recently they shut them all down. Only the bread and food departments still remain. The self-service restaurant is still offering Scottish salmon with chips and a piece of yellow lemon. God knows for how long that will continue. Dalir is carrying a bag full of things and they slowly walk back to the bicycle repair shop. Standing at the door, he does not hear anything and his heart gives up.

Are they all gone, leaving the shop empty?' He opens the door with a scared heart and he feels a huge sense of relief. The three boys are busy working in three corners. One is fixing a bike's chain that has come off. Another one is cleaning the toilet and the third one has a broom in his hand. Obviously he wanted to give a thorough cleaning to this place first. He feels very happy to see the boys working together.

Dalir puts the bag on the table and says, 'I would like to have a cup of tea with my cookie.'

'Cookies?'

Three boys jump on the plastic bags and the Chief has a simple uncomplicated smile on his face when he says, 'Quiet, boys. We have a visitor here.'

But it seems they do not care much about his remarks.

The boys have their cookies and, during lunch, they eat the bread and jam which has been sent for them by an angel from a farmhouse. There are even some fresh carrots and onions with some homemade yoghurt. Faris likes to have a piece of onion with his sandwiches and Breno can't do without yoghurt. Mongkut could fill up his tummy only with jam.

And Dalir understands all of it. He even knows how to fix the spokes of bikes. He knows the names of all those little bike parts. Above all, he knows the magical world of IND! The three asylum seeker boys are having the time of their lives, spending a day with a psychologist, who himself was once an asylum seeker and who got it and who has studied here and made it. Well, almost made it.

They do not know how the day passes. There was too much to do and even at the end of the day, they all feel that maybe they haven't done enough. The van driver Henk arrives with a microwave in his arms. He puts it on the table and says, 'Just found it on the street. Perhaps it still works. Perhaps it'll be useful here.'

Suddenly, seeing the Chief, he raises his eyebrows as he says in a curious tone, 'I thought – you said…!'

'Yes. I know.'

The Chief stops him. It is time to go home for all of them. The three boys have to be back at their camps in time. They have to have their evening meal there a lot earlier than ordinary people do.

After the boys have left, Henk says, 'Till then, Chief,' with a wink of his left eye. Dalir is still hanging around. 'Is there no one waiting for you, Dalir?' The Chief asks the question, knowing what the answer will be. Dalir stands up and says, 'Chief, my life does not mean much without her. She was the one that I have always waited for!'

But at one point Dalir also leaves and the Chief reflects on his whole day. He feels happy that finally he did not let his friends down. No. He must never do that. And he starts to think about Dalir differently. That little ape-man is not so bad after all. He knows a lot of things about many subjects.

Perhaps he could help the boys to make something out of their lives. Perhaps he will be able to teach them how to control their non-stop fear, which is making their clean hearts dirty. Of course not all of them will be accepted as asylum seekers by the government. But they must not lose hope. And they must not do crazy things, because they are not able to control their fright.

He closes the door of his friend's bicycle repair shop and, as he heads for his single room top floor apartment, he smiles again. This has been a good day. And like other working people, after the long hard working day, he is also going to his 'home' now.

He walks lightly towards his street with a plastic bag in his hand, as if he is carrying some shopping for his family. A family? Perhaps he will have one someday. He climbs all the steps of the narrow staircase and today, for the first time in his life, he does not find it tiresome. When he reaches his floor, he finds a new key hanging in his door.

The smell of new paint hits his nostrils. He

turns the key and goes in. But immediately he jumps out and looks around. Yes, it is his room. No mistake. But his room has changed! Is that magic? He enters inside his room again. He looks around in amazement. How is that possible? Who has done it? Who is the fairy this time? Or is it his brain playing a practical joke on him?

He looks around and goes to sit on his sofa-bed, which is a new one! The walls of his room are painted in bright light blue and there is a shaded lamp hanging from the ceiling. There is a new basin and a light is also hanging on top of it. And a mixing water tap! Would it be possible to wash his face and brush his teeth every morning with warm water from now on?

And in that corner? A white plastic door-like thing is hanging there. He goes over to it as if he is sleep-walking. And probably he is right. Behind the plastic door there is a tiny shower and a little low commode! A toilet in his room? A warm shower? He feels dizzy. He sits down on his sofa-bed and looks in front of him.

His grandfather is looking at him from a golden frame, which is now hanging on the bright blue wall! He nearly screams with fright. But he doesn't. There had been fairies around him in his earlier life and somehow they always knew exactly what he needed. Well, if one of them has taken his grandfather from his poster and has put him in a golden frame, then it is fine. He always wanted to do that someday. And that someday did not happen to him. But somehow it has happened now. He feels dreamy and tired.

He looks at the eyes of his grandfather and wants to have a discussion. 'Now, grandfather, now that the Trump guy has really got a place in the White House, how will life on the top of the Arizona Mountains be? And why is that place called the White House actually? Why not something else? Like Red house, Black house? Or even Yellow house?' How will this Trumpidian era end? Have you got any idea, wise old sage?

He feels very dizzy. His grandfather laughs at him and says reassuringly, 'Don't worry, my boy. Go to sleep now.'

But he just can't go to sleep. Something very unpleasant is happening here. He turns back to see his window and he shudders. There is an old floral curtain hanging at his window which is blocking the light from the sky outside. 'How dare they.' He feels angry and pulls down the curtains, throwing them out of his top floor window. How dare they cover his window! Now he comes to sit quietly on his new sofa-bed and pulls his old blanket from the corner.

He covers his body well and looks at his bare and open window as he murmurs, 'Look how nicely I have tucked myself in, *maman*! Now I am going to sleep, *maman*. And you can watch over me through the window, like a fairy or a star. Keep an eye on the night-hyenas. They must not touch me, *maman*! They mustn't hurt me anymore, *maman*! No more nightmares, *maman*. No more scary dreams!'

'The film is not done and the show must go on!'

15

The Lion's Den

There is a very careful knock on his door and someone is calling his name in a whisper. Perhaps it is the early morning wind, which does not want to rest. His eyes are still rather heavy and he does not want to open them yet. He wants to continue with his dream, which he is dreaming in his subconscious mind.

But the knocking has become impatient in the meantime and he has to wake up. He opens his eyes. The shadowy dim light from outside has created a mysterious atmosphere in his room. He sees the changes in his room again and once more his mind becomes perplexed. A dreamy world is moving like a white shadow in front of his eyes.

In a sleepy mood, he opens his door, expecting no one. But there is Henk standing at his door. He winks his left eye and says, 'Hurry.'

Henk runs down the steps and he runs after him, not knowing what is going on. It must all be happening in his sleep, he is thinking. The cold blast of early morning wind slaps him on his face and he is woken up properly by the cold breeze. He sees Henk's van is standing in the place where he is not allowed to park. He comes near the van and Henk winks again, to signal that he should climb into the van and make it snappy.

He sits next to the driver's seat and pushes his head against the headrest. He feels a soft touch of something on his neck and he almost jumps up out of fright. Henk laughs quietly and a tiny voice says, 'Hey, Chief, it is me, Lara. I am not Aleppo anymore.'

He looks behind him and sees the little angel bundled up in a thick blanket. Perhaps she has grown a lot in the meantime. That farmhouse has done her loads of good. She looks prettier than ever. Now his head becomes clear. Yes, she was going to come and Henk was going to bring her to him. And he has to take her to someone especially scary.

They drive around the canal and stop in front of the gate of a large house, which resembles a dark fortress of a witch in the Middle Ages. It is massive, dark and ugly. As soon as they have arrived, the huge iron gate opens automatically as if a giant has been waiting for them to do them a service. A cold voice orders, 'Put the blanket in the lift and you may leave now.'

Lara holds his hand with both her hands and he feels a fright passing through his heart again. In the meantime the lift has come down and it stops on the ground floor. Lara has tears in her eyes and, holding his hands tight, she begs, 'Don't let me go, Chief. Please don't. I am scared.'

He looks at her pleading face and feels rather confused. Lara is crying hard and says, 'Why can't I live with you? I don't eat much. I could also live on cold water like you do?'

He touches Lara's face softly with his cold fingertips and feels like he could live forever for a face like it! He feels he could fight a thousand battles to keep this fairy queen safe in her castle. He feels outraged and he shouts to the air, 'I'll come back for her. You better take good care of her. I'll certainly come back for this little precious one.'

He puts Lara in the lift and in the wink of an eye, it has gone up and disappeared.

He looks at the empty space of the lift and it seems as if nothing has ever been there but an iron zigzag gate. He looks at it and sits down in front of it. There is nothing to be seen but a vast black pit. Henk comes in to fetch him and holds out his two arms to lift him. He looks at him and breaks out in a loud cry, 'What have I done, Henk! What have I done to my little precious gem?'

Henk takes him out of the dark house and puts him in his van. Back at the front of his house, Henk just parks his car on the pavement. He does not care much now that, if the police should see this, they are not going to be amused at all. They both go up to his top floor room. Henk looks around and says, 'Now, Chief, you got a comfortable place here now, hey? Now you can live a decent life here. You have got a toilet and even a shower! What more could a guy want out of his life? A warm cup of coffee would be awfully effective at a moment like this.'

But his old electric kettle is gone and he never had any tea or coffee either. He doesn't care much about what Henk says. He is so overwhelmed with grief. His head is full with the image of the tears flowing from two emerald green eyes, asking for help while he was unable to bestow any. He feels helpless and immensely hopeless. And very, very sad!

He feels that he is going through a horrible nightmare again and he just has to reach the end line of it. He goes to lie down on his sofa-bed and doesn't even bother to cover himself with his blanket. Instead Henk takes it in his hands and says, 'Could you please move a bit, Chief? I haven't slept straight for many years now.'

Henk lies down next to him and as soon as he closes his eyes, he starts to snore like a storm.

His legs are crossed and folded together. Probably he doesn't dare to straighten up his legs for fear that he might get a cramp attack in his muscles. Or probably it has become a part of his habit of sleeping in the small space of a van, where he didn't enjoy having much legroom.

The Chief keeps his own eyes shut as if he does not want to hear anything or see anything. His mind is trying to reach Lara. How is Lara doing now? Is she very frightened? Has the quiet life of the farmhouse made her so weak? Of course she was not alone there. She had several people around, who loved her and cared for her. But they could not protect her. So she had to leave them and she came to him.

To him, the Chief of Amsterdam, who couldn't protect her either! He feels a great regret and shame at the same time. How could he not be able to save a sweet child like that with his two hands? How could he bring her to a Lion's Den? Extreme shame and remorse are suffocating his chest, as he says to the air, 'Lara, take care, little angel. I'll come to fetch you soon. I'll do that, love. Just give me a bit of time. I'll manage it somehow. Just trust me, little Lara. Trust me!'

And Lara does trust him. She dries her tears with the edge of her blanket and steps out of the lift as a tearless brave girl. She tries to observe this new place, which is huge. This is an extremely large room with high windows. There are lots of bookcases, which are full with many books on different subjects. But the shelves are all low. So low that a person in a wheelchair or a child will be able to pick up the books from the top shelves.

She moves closer to the bookshelves. Some books have titles written in Arabic, which she can barely read. Others are not familiar to her. In her confused state of mind, she had been thinking how exciting it would have been to be able to read a book with tales of a handsome prince and to go to the *Madrasa*, the so called Quran School, or a special school for girls of the kind they have in the cities, beyond her valleys, a luxurious city like Kabul or Ispahan.

She emits another frighteningly deep sigh and looks around a bit more. The other furniture in the house all reaches halfway up the wall. The top halves of the walls are full of paintings and colourful images. All the frames of the paintings are shining like gold, especially the larger ones. Some of them are indeed huge. Yet some are small and funny.

Now she is looking at a painting of a smiling goat playing a flute. And a lady in dark clothes with a strange smile. Another lady has a fish on her head. She feels like laughing. She does not like eating fish and her mother hates it. One day, she will tell her mother about this lady in the painting, who is carrying a fish-plate on her head. And there is another huge one! Several scary white men with thick moustaches hanging below their noses, in black clothes!

Most of the paintings are dark and in the dim light of the room, she can't really see much. This room is full of things. Still it feels empty. The room is so large that loads of things could still be added. Thick velvet curtains cover all the windows and the doors are automatically locked. Hardly anybody is visible so far. She shivers, thinking, 'Where am I?'

Suddenly a voice hits her ears, 'You are from a faraway place and have experienced many things. None of them were pleasant. What are you afraid of now?'

She looks back but sees no one. The same voice is laughing at her now.

'What you are hearing now is coming through an intercom. Soon you'll get used to it.'

A glass door opens and a wheelchair moves in the room and a figure which is sitting in it says, 'Follow me.'

She follows her. They pass a dark little passage and enter into a large room, which is all covered with dark green velvet curtains. A thousand lamps could be lit in this room. But no glimpse of light would be visible from the outside world!

The person in the wheelchair says, 'I keep all my valuables here in this room.'

She moves towards a large, finely hand-carved wooden portmanteau, which is painted pitch-dark black. She points at that black huge trunk and says, 'It is no use being sad about any guy on this planet.'

Suddenly Lara feels angry and, as if she is

wandering in a nightmare, she shouts to wake up and says, 'You are not supposed to talk like that about the Chief. He is just not like other guys. Soon he'll come back to fetch me. I know he will.'

Did the person on the wheelchair smile? She stops at the large portmanteau and gets up from her special wheelchair, while Lara looks at her in disbelief. She is a rather tall woman in her dark red decorated silk robe. Now she is walking towards the trunk and probably Lara wants to say something. But that person apparently can see everything from her back, as if she has two more extra eyes fixed in her back secretly.

And she says, 'Why should a woman walk, when there are guys to move her around? I am Lucretia and you must obey me in everything I say without any question. During the daytime you are free to walk in this room. But as soon as it gets dark, you must go inside that trunk, till I call you out. The nights are for the hyenas and during the daytime no one is to enter here.'

Lara looks frightened as she stares at the huge wooden trunk. Lucretia opens its lid and Lara looks inside. There are loads of curious things inside the trunk, including a nice little velvet quilt and a heart-shaped red pillow. Lucretia goes to the back of the trunk and pushes a button. One side of the plank moves and it shows a little doorway.

A person of her size would easily be able to move through it, using that door. Lucretia hangs a huge old lock on the lid of the trunk and says, 'This portmanteau was a gift from the king of Siam. He was a small king, who even wanted to give up his throne for me. Men! You must know that big kings do not need to give large gifts, because they are large themselves. Only the small ones need to show their large egos.'

Lara looks puzzled.

'From now on, you'll be free to move in this room alone and as soon as the evening approaches, you must go inside that trunk and fall asleep immediately. You can use the back sliding door that I showed you. There are holes in it and you are not going to suffocate. You can eat and drink during the daytime. Food will be brought here into this room. You may never open any curtains, whether it is day or night.'

Then she goes to sit on her wheelchair again, and disappears in her dark robe, like a ghost! Lara rolls her eyes and thinks aloud now, 'Where am

I? Oh Chief, what is happening to me? Take me home. Please come soon to take me away from here. I am so scared. Much more frightened than I was in that slave camp in Aleppo! This woman is not real, Chief. I'll tell you all about her.'

Lara looks at the huge trunk again. It is very high. Why would anyone build such an unusual trunk? But they were the kings and maybe those kings had loads of things to carry from one place to another. But what did that Siamese king have to give her in that huge trunk?

She wants to have a close look and goes back to the trunk. She pushes the button to open that hidden door and suddenly she hears a sound. She turns round in fright and sees a lift-like little thing coming down from the ceiling of the room. A voice says, 'This is your food for the whole day. There is a bathroom at the back of the wall of the trunk. Till tomorrow morning.'

Lara is now in a dreamland. Is this all real? She goes to the back of the huge trunk but she sees only a plain and shiny white wall. No sign of a door or open space. She starts pushing the wall with her palms and suddenly she feels a movement. The wall moves to one side and she finds herself in front of a very beautiful room.

She steps in and looks around. It must be a secret home of Aladdin! It is like 'open-sesame' and the magic door opens. But it is only a bathroom! She does not recognise all the things that are there. But all of them are shining like gold. Or are they all made of gold? There is a wash basin and bath and also a shower. There are European clothes for a girl of her size!

Perhaps someone has the same taste concerning clothes as she herself. She looks at the trousers and the sweaters. They are all expensive and pretty. A pair of golden slippers too! Perhaps she has landed in a magic world. She feels like taking a shower. A bath might take too much water and maybe Lucretia is not going to like it. She would rather take a good shower and have her breakfast.

Suddenly she feels a pang in her tummy. Her nostrils are creating an imaginary sweet smell of homemade fresh bread. Ah! That farmhouse, which had been her home for a while! How happy she was there with all of them together. And being with Posette.

In that farmhouse she had been eating too much. She had been in the kitchen most of the time, helping either Aaf or Posette. Tears roll in her eyes now. Her heart breaks for the farmhouse. And Posette. Her dear Posette! How she is longing to see her and to be in her arms again. Or to lie down next her and talk about the Chief! She wants to cry for both of them and says, like a prayer, 'Oh Chief! And oh dear cousin Posette, I miss you two so much. A devilish enchantress has captivated me. And I can't run away, unless the Chief comes to free me and take me away.'

She promises to herself that one day she will be out of this fake situation and then she will tell everybody all and everything about this sorceress, that she is not a crippled woman at all, who is sitting in her wheelchair and ordering people to push her around! She is phoney. Very seriously false. If only the Chief could see her now and could feel her fright!

'The film is not done and the show must go on!'

16

The Ark of Isodore

The Chief is standing outside now and looking at the houses on the other side of the canal. Which house was that one? In which one is the witch keeping his precious gem? Now in bright morning light, he can't recognise that dark house exactly. It is as if it was an enchanted house, which existed at night and then disappeared completely as soon as daylight had blessed the city. Or was it all a nightmare? Did he really bring Lara to a she-devil?

He lets go a remorseful sigh. Why has his life become so complicated now? He was alone and he had nothing. And he didn't care about not having anything. Now, he also has nothing. Yet, he feels something like responsibility in his chest. Lara, that little angel, has taken away all his solace. He must protect Lara from all the evil spirits that are hunting for her. He wants to say a prayer for her, but only says, 'Little child, keep yourself safe and calm. I'll be there soon.' He rolls his red steamy eyes and turns around.

It is time to go to his work. The bicycle shop is waiting for him. The boys will be there. He does not know anything about bikes. That Dalir guy knows a lot. But he is a psychologist and he has a very important job with the government. What's more, he's got a wife and children. Probably a very troublesome wife. He seems like a nice guy who has lost his way. But he is not going to come to their bicycle repair shop every day. Isodore's back is no good. His physiotherapist has advised him to take rest. He feels sorry that he has never really learned a trade well, so that he could teach someone how to be a professional.

He arrives at the bicycle repair shop and feels relieved to see that there is no one waiting for him. He opens the huge wooden door and goes inside. A large amount of daylight is coming through the top skylight now. This place is so enormously large. One could make a theatre out of this place. Or a kindergarten. Or a library. Or perhaps a café? But no. No!

This is the place of Isodore. And he loves to repair bikes. Repairing broken bikes has been the only challenge in his life. Now he is ill and can't hire professional help to do his job. He never has a lot of spare money. And his long-time girlfriend Berenguela is not coming here either. He produces a heartbroken sigh and looks up, thinking, 'Hey Old Man up there, why did you create me like this? Is this punishment for a sin that I committed in a previous life?'

Suddenly the whole of the bicycle repair shop is flooded with bright sunrays and it is as if he hears a voice which says, 'Despair not. The film is not done and the show must go on!' He shudders in fear. He feels that he is experiencing a theophany of some kind.

The huge wooden door opens and he hears a voice, 'Look who I have found, Chief.'

It is the Syrian refugee boy with Dalir. Right after them the other two refuge boys come in. He feels so happy to see them as if he could hold them to his chest and give them a bear hug. Instead he smiles and says, 'Good to see you, Dalir. Don't you have to work today?'

'No, Chief. I have taken a few weeks of holiday,'

he says meekly. The Syrian Faris looks curious. 'Holiday, Uncle Dalir? With your wife and kids? I have never had a holiday in my whole life. Can I also come with you and Aunty on your holiday? It will be awfully nice to meet my new cousins.'

Dalir smiles and says, 'You may call me 'uncle' when we are alone. But not in public. And my wife is not your aunt. Just the same, my kids are not your cousins. People here will not understand it and you might get into trouble with the IND for having an uncle living here in the Netherlands and not telling them about it. They will ask you thousands of questions about one of your imaginary 'uncles' and in the end they will call you a liar! This country is a lonely planet and one cannot create a family just because one wants to have the pleasure of feeling the warmth of having a kin in one's heart.'

Faris looks sad but Mongkut smiles at him with a friendly gesture and says, 'Don't be sad, Faris. The psychologist is right. It is not Asia or the Middle East. In those countries, there are mothers and every mother is your mother. But here, they will be scared if you should use that intimate term with them.'

Now the Syrian boy looks more confused than

ever as he says, 'Do you know how difficult it is to call an elderly person by their first name? Do we call anybody by their first or second names for that matter, in our part of the world?'

Dalir smiles and says, 'You'll get used to it. We all do.'

They all have a silent moment now. They are reflecting on the situation. In warm countries, relationships are based on family terms. So, your friends' parents are like your own parents. Your neighbours are your aunts and uncles and cousins. But here in Europe and especially in colder countries, it is friendships that you can count on. In an Asian society, you cannot call an elderly person by name. That would be a serious insult to the person in question.

But in this country, you are asked to call them by name, if and when you are friends with them. In that way, the European person in question feels less burdened and more comfortable. It is friendship which counts in a society like this. Well, that is if you are lucky to have someone to call a 'friend'. Breno Morales is quiet all the time and then says, 'I had lots of friends on the streets of my home town.'

The conversation has turned heavy and the

Chief looks at Dalir and says, 'Perhaps you can ask your wife if she would like to take Faris with you, on a holiday?'

'Chief, my wife is already having her holiday, somewhere in a country on the border of Iran, with her family. You see I only take time off when she is gone.'

The other two boys also get involved in their conversation and Mongkut says, 'Woman. Too much trouble. No wife – life is good.'

Dalir shakes his head in acknowledgement and the Chief nods his head, which could mean, 'Is that so?', or, 'Let it be.'

But he has something else on his mind. He has to find a way to help his friend. Isodore might come today to see the situation in his bicycle repair shop. If only they could give him some good news, something to cheer him up. He makes some coffee in the paper cups and searches for something little to go with it. The boys have all taken their sandwiches with them. They too have realised that the bicycle repair shop cannot be charitable to them all the time. They know that they have to be careful too with Isodore's shop.

They all are sitting with their tea, when Henk

also arrives. He looks fresh and happy. 'Ha, Chief, what a place you got. I took a shower at your place and now I feel very clean. Only, I am in need of clean underwear. And next time I'll find some towels for you. By the way, I took some bread and cheese from the neighbour guy. In fact he was going to bring it to your apartment for you. So I took it. Let's have some decent breakfast, hey?'

The three asylum seeker boys do not feel like grabbing the bread. Neither do they look at the cheese. They are all reflecting on their situation. They feel that they all have such a miserable life that they even can't give Isodore a helping hand. They are just not good enough to find a way out for that good-hearted charitable soul.

The Chief looks at them and says, 'Have you guys noticed what a grand place this is?'

They do not understand exactly what he means. But they all agree that it is really a grand place.

'Well then, imagine, just imagine, this place belongs to you. What could you turn this place into?'

Before the Chief can finish his words, Mongkut has a large smile on his face, which makes his flat nose even flatter and he says, 'But this place is not our place. It is the place of Uncle Isodore.'

The other two boys join him, saying that since the place belongs to Isodore, there is no point in them thinking about things that are not going to happen.

Suddenly there is a nasty voice inside the bicycle repair shop. With clear disdain, it says, 'So? You may think like that. This place does not belong to Isodore. He is just like me, a tenant of the 'madam', of whom we all are tenants.'

They all look at him with a curious surprise. He shakes his head as if some bugs are eating up his brain.

He is now itching his head with all his ten fingers as he continues, 'Yes, I mean that witch of the dark castle. Probably the whole city belongs to her. But maybe not.'

The Chief looks at him with disdain and, with an irritated voice, he asks, 'Hey Visigoth, how did you find this place? And what are you doing here?'

Visigoth turns almost violent. 'How did I find this place? Is this a secret place? I was ordered by the queen to bring you some breakfast every morning. And also lunch and dinner for that matter. But where do I bring it, if I don't know your whereabouts, hey? So, I followed this empty-headed driver of yours. And now what do I see? The ape-man! This stupid nut is here to double-cross me. Hey? Are you here to meet up with that slut behind my back?'

Before he has finished his last sentence, an enormous blow falls on his nose and he sits down on the floor, bleeding. Dalir looks at him and says, 'Thank you, Chief. I have always wanted to do that.'

The three boys clap their hands and say, 'Look mister tall guy, we were discussing a serious problem and you just buzzed in and started a fight with Chief?'

Dalir goes to the toilet space and comes back with a piece of wet tissue and laughs.

'I see lots of improvement here. The toilet is clean?'

The boys smile with pride and Breno says, 'Yeah, We have learned it at COA. We all have to keep that place clean in turns. So we have planned to clean this place every day, bit by bit. So the boss will be happy. We'll make this place nice for him.'

Visigoth makes a face at him and mocks him with a strange monkey-like gesture.

'Aha? So you make a clean shop for him? And what good is that going to do to him? Is he going to make money with a clean shop? Are people coming here to see his clean bicycle repairing palace? He needs money, like we all do. And that slut is gone and I am ruined. My life is ruined. And now I am being ordered to take care of this unholy Indian of the Arizona Mountains. Why don't you buy a servant for yourself, hey?'

'And why don't you buy a soul to keep inside your chest?' the Chief says carelessly.

'Aha! You are talking about souls? The priests in those ugly villages of Poland talk about souls, while they sell their own little boys to dirty old pigs, who use them for pederasty. They sell their own children for a bottle of Irish whiskey? Where is their soul kept then? And that slut? A doctor who came to Western Europe, to earn more money as a sex worker in the red-light district? Can you imagine that? Does that whore have a soul in her harlot's chest?' Visigoth's mouth is now full of spit and he looks at the Chief as if he wants to start a physical fight.

This time Dalir goes to throw another blow on his nose. But the Chief stops him by holding him from behind. Dalir sits down on a broken plastic chair and looks at Visigoth with disdain, saying, 'Look, you frivolous man. Look at those three boys now. They are all suffering from 'Aboulia' and why is that? Not because they were only abused physically, but also mentally and sexually.'

'Do you think that those kids who are living in those beautifully decorated houses are all happy? Do you know that they are also the victims of the lust of their own male relatives? Like their own father, step-father, mother's partners or boyfriends? Have you got any idea how many kids cannot sleep at night because they are afraid of their dirty old male family members? And are they all sold for a bottle of alcohol? Or the need for money?'

Visigoth dries his blood now with a tissue and shouts back, 'Those kids are stupid. Why don't they shout out loud, when they know that they are going to be abused?'

Dalir suddenly stands up and jumps on top of him. 'How dare you talk like that? Have you ever been a kid? Did you enjoy your own daddy molesting you? Or your uncles tasting your testicles?'

The Chief pulls Dalir back and looks at Visigoth with strong antipathy and says, 'You are a man without any soul, Visigoth Wamba. From now on, you must never say that the kids are stupid. Because they are not. They don't shout for help, because they don't want to hurt their mothers. Because they want to protect their mothers and they want to see their mothers' smiling faces all the time! So, they make a sacrifice of their own life and they keep quiet. Yes, they smile to their mothers and they keep silent!'

Visigoth is still cleaning his painful wounds and keeping his head down. The Chief looks at the boys, who seem extremely sad. He clears his thoughts and says, 'Look, all of you. Ignore that guy and listen to me. We must help Isodore. He is ill and he has got no money. This shop is all he got. Even if it is a rented place, still we could do something here, which will help him. But what could we do here? There are not enough repairs going on. He can't live from that profession. We must find a way, which will give him an opportunity to be happy again. We are his friends and we must help him.'

'Well, you can't change this place to turn it into something else. You'll need permission for that. And that will cost you all of your lifetimes. And at the end, all of you will get a heart attack. Or end up in a bedlam. You stupid little nuts, can't you see that I am broke too? And I am also trying to change my job and trying to do something else. But who will hire me? Who will give an ex-convict a decent job, who is known here as a pimp?'

Visigoth's anger turns into desperate tears and he is now lamenting. 'We all want to have the best for ourselves. Sometimes we make mistakes and we take the wrong paths. But who cares? There is no one to show us the right way.'

There is the sound of a cough and they all look behind them. Isodore is standing there and they feel a sort of embarrassment in themselves. How long has he been standing there? They have been discussing his situation and probably he has heard it all. It is not nice for him to know that others are discussing his misfortunes, while he is not there.

Isodore comes close to them and sits down on his broken plastic chair with difficulty. He looks at all of them and smiles. 'This place certainly looks a lot better now. And when I have so many friends, why should I worry about anything at all? Hey, friends, what possibilities could this place have? What do you think?'

They all look at each other. The three asylum

seeker boys now realise when and how you make friends in a cold country and exactly when you belong to a friend. They feel so overwhelmed and important now. Faris says, 'You know, boss, in Syria, when you got nothing to eat, you go to sell tea on the streets. We could all sell tea and coffee for you?'

'Yeah, we could sit on the pavement with a can of tea and some paper cups? Like we do in Asia.'

Mongkut smiles now.

'But it is not Asia, Mongkut. Here in Europe, you need permission from the authorities to do anything you might want to do.' Breno's voice sounds profoundly sad.

Isodore gestures to Breno to come near him and says, 'My little friend, first we all have to decide what exactly we want to do. First we have to agree on that. And then we'll have to see how to get permission from the city bosses for it. Now, the idea of selling tea is a very good one. But I am afraid; we can't do that on the streets. How can we do it, Visigoth?'

Isodore looks at their faces.

Probably Visigoth feels as if his tongue has got arrested somewhere in his throat. In a frightened voice he says, 'Look, Isodore, my business is also finished. But that is nothing for you to be troubled about.' He looks at the Chief as if asking to rescue him.

'Isodore, we all know how much you feel for this place. This bicycle repair shop has been your whole life's partner. But things have changed through the years. All those exotic shops are gone. Under every house, each and every basement is either a whorehouse or coffee shop. You don't want to start a brothel, do you?'

They all laugh when the Chief stops.

'No. Chief, we don't want to start a brothel. With all due respect to the world's oldest profession, we don't want to do that. But something else. Of course I'll miss the bicycle tyres and oil and grease. I'll miss the dirt of this place. My heart will break to change this place into something else. But it is up to you. Whatever my friends will decide for me, I'll agree.'

The Syrian refugee boy whispers into the ear of the Chief and says, 'Chief, listen to me, we can sell coffee in here. In that way, we'll be rich too.' Perhaps Isodore has heard him and he thinks for a while and in a very sad tone he says, 'Okay then.

We shall have a coffee shop here, my friends.'

Coffee! The black drug, which is legal everywhere.

'But how about the permission from the Mayoral office? That will take you an eternity,' Visigoth shouts with unconcealed pleasure and guffawing at the same time.

Isodore looks at the Chief and says, 'What do you think, Chief? Would it be possible to get permission to make a café out of this place, out of this mess?' The Chief is silent now. His mind is wandering about a wheel, the wheel of fortune!

'The film has not ended yet. And the show must continue!' Who has planted this phrase in his mind?

'The film is not done and the show must go on!'

17

Avant Garde

'Is this house number 777? Or am I mistaken?'

The Chief looks up and meets the eye of a postman with a bag full of envelopes. He looks like a cheerful sort of guy in his orange uniform. He has letters for Isodore from a couple of debt collector companies. The so-called loan-sharks engage these sorts of companies to bring borrowers to their ends.

He feels like punching the postman's nose. But he realises that it is not his fault. The postman is just doing his job in delivering letters for a nasty company and he himself is not the bailiff. How can a person ever take the job of a bailiff? Those people must possess a very sordid conscience. He feels upset for Isodore, yet he must accept the registered letter and sign for it. He thanks the postman and says, 'Yes. This is number 777 and you may leave the post with me.'

There are some other letters too. The three frightened boys maintain deep silence while the Chief talks with the postman. When the postman has left, Faris opens his mouth, 'I hate letters. I hate postmen. They always bring bad news.'

Breno sounds even bitterer as he supports the comments of Faris. 'Yeah. Always letters from IND, stating you may leave this country, because your story is not true. Your documents are false and your –'

'Yeah, yeah. And your arsehole does not show any sign of being abusively raped. And there is no clear evidence that your mother's husband starved you till you agreed to let him abuse you whichever way he wanted. You have to give clear answers to horrible questions like, how did you experience the abuse of your step-father? Did you let him enjoy your arsehole? Did you suck his male organ? Was that all a 'p–' to 'p–' relation? Did you enjoy it yourself?'

His vocal cords become weak as he continues, 'There is no proof that you had to dress up like a girl and dance like a hooker for those dirty old perverts, who would buy you for a night and show their abusive power over you. You could not prove any of those disgusting events. You could not make it clear to them that all you wanted at those moments was to die. You wanted to die out of shame! The memories of the horrifying shame constricts your throat, making you unable to tell the tale of the maltreatment! So you are a liar and you may leave this country right now!'

Mongkut's whole body is shaking as he breaks into violent tears. Both Faris and Breno go to hold him in their arms and try to comfort him.

'We know, dear brother! We know how deeply it hurts and you don't need to be ashamed of it. We all are the victims of abuse and they are not supposed to believe us! We are too many refugees with too many stories. It is their job to listen to us. They were not there with us to experience the brutality we went through and so they can't make a distinction between truth and falsehood. But we are young boys and we have hopes!'

'Yes. You are right. And they will wait till you reach the age of eighteen. Because by then, you are an adult, a grown up man, and no-one is responsible for you but you yourself. Then they will allow you to experience the outside world. They will set you free on the street to be an adventurer. That will be in the summer and outside temperatures will be agreeable and you will survive on the streets somehow.'

They all look at an extremely frazzled Dalir, who has just arrived at the bicycle repair shop and has been listening to their conversations agog.

He takes his usual broken plastic chair and continues to throw some more information to the boys.

'Then suddenly the climate will turn harsh on you by lowering the temperature. It will turn cold and rainy and you will need a shelter to keep yourself warm. What will you do then? You will have no choice and a dirty old beast will always know how to find you! You are eighteen and yet vulnerable, a perfect prey for disgusting lusts. The law can't protect you from those dirty hands, because you are an adult by now. That is the how the story often runs!' Dalir explains clearly the frightening future for these boys.

The three boys are awfully quiet now, as if they have forgotten that they are here and there might still be hope for them. This conversation is soon going to take the form of fiery arguments and that should not take place in the bicycle repair shop of the very kind Isodore, who is ill and can't work hard anymore.

Moreover, that kind man has no money and he is deep in debt. Only he himself knows how much he owes to whom. But he can't pay any cent. Probably, he has also not paid his rent, like the rest of them. So one day, this bicycle repair shop of Isodore will be closed and he will simply be thrown out of this grand place. What a pity that they can't help him.

The three boys come near to him and say, 'Chief, can't we work somewhere else to make some cash for the boss, so that he could at least pay his rent? We can work hard and we want to help him.' The Chief looks at all of their faces and he smiles a sad smile. How wonderfully kind-hearted these three boys are!

They must have inherited this soft humane character from their biological parents. Their parents are lucky to have them, no matter how maddening their present situation is. He emits a deep sigh and says, 'There is an Old Man up there and he is watching us. Let's wait for his mercy.'

They hear the whirring sound of the tyres of

the van and slowly the driver Henk comes in, with two shopping bags in his hands. Usually the three boys always rush towards him, to carry the bags. But today, they remain busy with their own work.

'What has happened to this place? Everybody is so quiet? Anybody's mother-in-law died?'

But no one reacts to Henk's joke.

Nevertheless he continues, 'Huh! Bad letters everywhere. Beren has got some horrible letters this morning too and some bailiff guys came to take everything from the farmhouse. Beren is very upset and Isodore has gone there to comfort her. Some money must be paid in seven days' time! Just imagine, only seven days and where the heck are they going to collect that amount of money from? Posette has got no single cent either.'

Henk shakes his head in a sign of bravado and says, 'Only Aaf. That clever maid has been saving all her salary for years now and she has given it all to Beren to save the farm. You see, that farm is actually her home too. But there is no exit for Isodore. He is completely broke. This place will have to be shut down soon.'

Henk does not sound sad or disappointed. He explains plain facts, the way they are, plain and straight. It seems he does not realise what exactly he has been talking about.

Isodore comes in with his usual good mood and smiles at everyone, 'Hello friends, how are the bikes today? Oh, the postman has visited me already? How many letters are there today? Well, we'll have to face it one day, won't we?'

He gives the letters to Henk and says, 'Please open them one by one and read them aloud. I hate reading letters. That has always been Beren's job. But now she is occupied with baby Ivan. You know how engaging babies can be!'

Henk sits down on the plastic chair and opens the first letter from one of the debt collectors' offices. It says that, if he fails to pay within seven days, one of the bailiffs of the debt collectors' company will visit his place in person and will remove all the valuables from his property.

They all want to laugh aloud hearing this statement.

But then they look around the place and realise it is no joke. This place is still full of valuable things. Broken bikes are not something that you can just get rid of? They also have souls. Some of them were made and given a shape here, in this shop!

And the metallic parts of the bicycles are valuable too. Those metals have living souls as well. They are the metallic soul-mates of Isodore.

Now Henk picks up an expensive looking envelope, which is large and thick, bearing the monogram of the Mayor's office. He looks at the beige-coloured and embossed envelope suspiciously and says, 'A very strange letter. Should I open it? Or throw it in the canal?'

'No. Just open it and read it. Perhaps it is an order to close this place. You see, the whole neighbourhood has changed. Everything is shining and gleaming. This place does not fit in with all those glitters.'

A heartbroken deep sigh comes out of his chest as Isodore turns his sad face to hide his tears.

A reluctant Henk opens the envelope and his eyes become wide. He forgets to read and the three boys scream at him. 'Now go on, Uncle Henk. We are not waiting for ages to hear some bad news from a cruel bailiff-office?'

Henk mumbles inside his mouth as if he has forgotten how to speak. 'Isodore, I mean, Boss, you got the permission from the office of the Mayor to turn this place into a café!'

All of their mouths are agape now as Henk continues, 'And you may call this place, 'Chief's Café, Amsterdam'.'

They all look at each other. Why 'Chief's Café'? They are extremely puzzled. It seems so bizarre! So incredible! It must be a mistake! Or a cruel joke by someone. A permission letter for someone who has got absolutely not a single coin in his ripped-off pocket! And this place does not even belong to him! Although he has rented the place from someone, Isodore has been a sort of owner here for ages now. So the permission is rightfully given to him to turn the place into a café. But why on earth is the mayoral office suggesting that this new café should be called 'Chief's Café'? For what reason are they making things complicated?

In the meantime two tall and dashing-looking guys in fresh and shiny expensive suits come in and ask for Isodore. The three boys were looking at their suits and shoes, thinking that they will never ever have the pleasure even to touch such suits in their entire lifetime. Do the presidents of their own countries have such expensive clothes? And those shoes? One could buy a house in their village with the price for one pair of those elegant shoes.

But all their expensive clothes and the smell of exotic aftershave cannot hide their true nature. They look as if they are the twin brothers of Satan himself. Even their identical red-and-white dotted ties look phoney. Who are these two guys? Who possesses such a dirty heart that they can send them here to hurt someone like their boss Isodore?

A very puzzled Isodore makes clear with a gesture that it is he who is called Isodore. The boys push two greasy chairs over for the two shiny guys and they sit down on the chairs, looking greatly pleased, as if they are having the honour of sitting in the court of the Mughal emperor Akbar the Great. They look around the place and smile from ear to ear.

They cough to clear their throats. In the meantime the boys have brought them two cups of tea in used paper cups. They start sipping their tea and say to Isodore, 'Now Mr de Saville, or may we call you just Isodore? Our friend Isodore, we are here to invest some money in your business. We mean, in your café. We gathered the news that you have already obtained permission from the office of the Mayor and you are all equipped to start this place soon. The money will be in your bank account before noon and shall we say we'll be able to sit here and have a cup of coffee in a week's time?'

'Yes. Coffee with cream. Herbal tea of course. Cheese cubes. And of course music. Live music and dancing. Young dancers from the dancing schools. Ach yeah, those young ones. How they love to dance throughout the evening, almost for nothing! Their young skin is so soft and they don't mind many things. That is the fun of it.' The other guy murmurs as if he doesn't want anyone to hear his thoughts.

'In a week's time?' one of the boys shouts, in fear.

Isodore is still speechless. Probably he has turned mute because of the unexpected events.

'Yes. We would love to hear some live music and some dancing girls are always nice of course.'

The two guys now look at the Chief inquiringly, as if they need a definitive answer from him. Their voices are cold now. Their eyes are shining like small rodent's eyes.

The Chief feels that he must reassure Isodore and he says, 'Didn't God create this planet earth for us in seven days? There are seven seas and seven days in a week. Our house number is three times seven. Of course you'll have your coffee here after seven days. Black coffee and herbal tea. No drugs, no smoking. It will be a clean place for sophisticated minds. And there will be live music here too. But no dancing girls. No!'

The two guys finish their tea and get up to say good day to all of them, shaking their hands in such a way as if all of the wretched workers of the bicycle repair shop are directors of a large company, listed on the stock exchange.

As soon as they are gone, the three boys start to scream with joy. They jump around Isodore and say, 'Look, Boss, our luck has changed.'

'The almighty Allah had listened to my prayers,' says Faris in a devotional tone.

'But, Chief, how are these things happening? Is it real? Or are we all dreaming, Chief?'

Isodore sounds as if he is indeed having a dream. Only Henk shouts, 'Don't just sit there, boys. We have got a lot to do. It is only seven days that we have got in our hands? We must find people to clean up this mess. Good builders and electricians. Furniture. Oh my God!' Henk collapses on the floor, creating a very loud noise. This must be the very first time in his life that he has passed out with positive excitement.

'So, so. Ha! He has passed out? Good for him. And you, Chief? And you, Isodore? What do you think about all this? I mean – of course you are not going to tell me how all of a sudden your luck has changed. Though I have a suspicion about that. But I am not bothered. Not yet? I am not jealous the way I should be. But, I am angry, as angry as I can be. Yes, I am very, very angry. So angry, that I could make this place go up in flames in no time. And why not?' Visigoth laughs at them like a hardened criminal.

'You have never shown any respect for the law, Visigoth.'

The very tired Isodore is looking at him without any interest.

'Law? What has the law ever done for me? How many years will a lunatic get, for reducing your place to ashes? Isn't jail better than being on the streets? At least there is a TV in your cell to kill the time and they make you watch CNN as a daily punishment.'

Visigoth seems determined to pick a physical

fight. He looks wild and his fingers are searching for something that he could kill right now.

No one says anything to him. Then Dalir gets up and says, 'Look, Visigoth, I am still your therapist, right?'

'So what?' Visigoth shouts at him.

'So I can write a report about you stating you are a danger being on the streets and your head is not good enough to continue the business which you have been running. The human rights organizations are not going to like it. You see, sex-workers have united worldwide and you are nothing compared with their collective power. They will put you away forever. Remember Johannesburg? Do they have TV too in their jails?'

Dalir looks at him with knife-sharp eyes.

Visigoth shouts at him and grabs his throat.

'You dirty shrink. You think you can do that? I'll kill you before you say another word to frighten me.'

A very calm Dalir looks him in the eye and says, 'Look, Visigoth, you can try to hurt me. But that is not going to help you. Just get off me and listen carefully. You may be able to make a profit out of the situation.'

Visigoth lets him go and in a mocking tone, asks, 'Profit? These two shits of guys have got money and permission to start a coffee-shop here and I'm going to make a profit out of their good fortune?'

Dalir goes to sit down on his chair. He smiles at Visigoth and says, 'Yeah. They got the money and the permission. But they only have seven days in their hands, right? Doesn't that itself sound to you like a punishment? Now, without your help, how can they ever manage that?'

Visigoth is now looking for a place to sit too. His mouth is agape as he asks, 'How can I be a help to them? And why should they accept my offer?'

Dalir smiles generously towards all of them and looks calmly at Visigoth.

'Remember who you are? You belong to the clan of the great warriors.'

'Yeah, he belongs to a clan who were killers. No doubt his body is full of killer genes. Ha ha ha!'

Visigoth jumps up from his chair and shouts, 'Who said that? Who dares to utter such insults about my ancestors? They were warrior soldiers.'

He looks menacingly at the three boys and makes a big fist with both his hands. His long face looks as if it is burning at a temperature of five hundred degrees.

In the meantime, the Chief goes to the boys and stands in front of them as if to shield them from the wrath of Visigoth.

'Well, Visigoth, killers and warriors are just the same. Don't you ever dare to hurt these boys. Now either you listen to your therapist or you may leave.'

Then the Chief looks at the boys and says, 'Friends, we got loads to do and there is not enough time.'

Dalir gestures to Visigoth to sit down and he goes to sit on the chair again.

'Now you have an opportunity to show off your energy and courage. There is loads to be done in a week's time. You know lots of people in the city who are involved in different businesses, right? We need contractors, builders, furniture, decorating equipment. And first of all, we need to clean up this place.'

Dalir looks at Isodore thoughtfully now and says softly, 'We cannot throw away these precious things of Isodore. That will break his heart. Let's imagine that one good day, and I am sure that day will come, Isodore will reopen his bicycle repair shop and he will have all his things around him. So, everything that is in this place, we must keep somewhere and move it all carefully, so it doesn't get lost.'

Suddenly Isodore gets up. He goes to hug smallish Dalir and he doesn't try to stop his tears. 'Dalir, my brave friend! My brave brother! Forgive me for not taking you seriously before. How could you read my mind?'

Dalir dries his own wet eyes and says, 'Detecting a man's pain is my job, my brave friend and my brave brother!'

'The film is not done and the show must go on!'

18

The Three Musketeers

A large signboard in bright orange is hanging over the large wooden door, reading *Chief's Café, Amsterdam*, which has replaced the old signboard of Isodore's bicycle repair shop. The renovation has started under the supervision of Visigoth, who is acting as the boss now. He has hired all the builders that he knows. It seems he knows quite a few building companies, where most of the workers are foreigners.

There is the Bulgarian builder Stanimir, who actually is a great biologist in his homeland, and now works as a bathroom specialist. He is accompanied by his partner Irina. This Tatarina is actually a famous opera singer and in most parts of Russia her name is uttered with respect and pride. Her family had good connections with the family of Nureyev.

The two families were connected by music, as she pointed out that her grandmother was a great pianist. When he was a little boy, the Nureyevs would send their boy Rudolf Khametovich to her grandmamma, for taking dancing lessons.

Then there is the Russian electrical engineer Anatoly Manikin, who is actually a painter, whose main job was to make official portraits of high-ranking functionaries in the Soviet era. Now he works as an electrician for an acquaintance of his, who is also from Moscow and who is now running a building company. All the Russian immigrants are hanging around him as if he is the magnet for them. The building world of the Netherlands cannot hammer one single nail anywhere without him knowing about it.

This guy, who is called Mecho, is very lucky in making money and he controls all of the workers from Eastern Europe. Without the unwritten permission of Mecho, no one will dare to engage themselves in any work whatsoever. He is certainly not a control freak. Not at all. He ran away from Soviet Russia and the reason was that he did not feel that there was any need to control him. He has always been a law-abiding citizen.

He studied English classical novels in depth, which had been secretly translated into Russian by some crazy people and he secretly nurtured a mind of his own, adapting the character of a British phlegmatic snob. This Mecho studied linguistics and wanted to make a name for himself as a linguist and teacher. But it must be his bad karma that his students thought him a stolid fellow and pretty soon his classrooms were empty. He has been a promotor of Cyrillic languages and he has a great respect for anyone who at least tries to talk one or two words of his mother-tongue, Russian.

Above all, there were four Vladimirs of different shapes and sizes. One is Vovaye, one is simply Vova. And there is Vadya, who likes to dance the Polka. The last one is called the 'tall Vlad'. This Vlad always keeps quiet in the group. His head is always bent down and his face is shaded by a dark-green army cap, which he keeps on his head twenty-four hours a day. Vovaye graduated as a mechanical engineer from a renowned university in Moscow and worked with several governments as a top class engineer. But suddenly he lost his job and couldn't find anything else to do.

His wife Ludmila, who was working as a nurse

in a small village hospital, has always been a great admirer of the West. She met a Dutch guy in her village, who was holidaying and staying in her neighbour's barn, in exchange for helping them milk the goats. They bumped into each other accidentally in that barn. That meeting took about thirty minutes, lying on top of each other on the warm hay and when she left to go to pick up her child, he even kissed her on her lips. So one fine day, she left the village for the free Western world, with that guy, taking her only daughter Nelly, who was then about four years old.

Ludmila's love-affair did not last that long, because her new boyfriend couldn't get used to a child nagging around him all the time. And the child could not stand him butting in all the time in the strictly private affairs of mother and daughter. But that broken relationship did not leave any mark on Ludmila. She did not find that Dutch lover very romantic anyway. He was a straightforward hard-working guy and, after a few months, he did not show much involvement with their closed lives anyway.

After a couple of months living together with him, she told her little daughter Nelly that her lover was someone who most probably had a farmer's background and who was smart enough to be able to study a bit. But that was it. It was time to move on. Why water a plant which has no roots that are attached to the soil? Better save the water in the watering can, for the next plant.

She did not discriminate against farmers. But once a farmer, always a farmer. Green grass will always be for him just grass for the cows and sheep to feed and never a lush green field to walk in, or sit on to smell its fresh scent. Or simply lie down on, when the midday summer sun turns everything golden and warm in such a manner, when a living soul will long to touch the soil with its own heart.

So she applied for asylum to the Dutch government with her little daughter Nelly and then they went to live on their own. Her Dutch ex-lover helped her to move into her new room and he even built a thin partition wall to divide the room into two, so that mother and daughter would have some privacy, which is a number one necessity in Dutch society. In the meantime her husband Vovaye, who was still her lawfully wedded husband, came to see their daughter.

And little Nelly did not let her father go. So now

Vovaye is working with Mecho's building group too and he is an artist in his own right. He makes beautiful things from glass and lead and there is nothing that he cannot do. He is in great demand inside the circuit of the building companies. Now, he has also come to make the café ready within seven days!

Visigoth has made it clear to all of them that he is the manager here and they all have to obey him. He is shouting non-stop to the three asylum seeker boys to get them to understand that those rotten bikes will have to be gone before he gets back from his lunch. Before the renovation started, the boys were engaged to clean up the bicycle parts and collect them in huge cardboard boxes.

There are too many of the junk boxes and they are trying to pile them against a corner wall. The boxes are becoming heavy and they need some more boxes to put all the parts in systematically. The others are gone for lunch and those three are left to keep an eye on the place. Soon Isodore will be coming to tell them where exactly they should bring these boxes with parts. Henk suggested that a corner of the barn of Beren's farmhouse would do the trick. But Isodore has said nothing. Now, they simply have to wait for their boss.

They are leaning against the piled-up full boxes, trying to stretch their arms and legs. Mongkut tries to show off by making a Kung Fu movement and the kick hits the wall. Suddenly a huge cracking sound deafens their ears and they shudder with fright. The wall gives in and a little passage is visible inside!

It all looks dark and they think for a moment what to do. They are still trembling with fear. Holding each other's hands, they go inside the cave-like thing. It is very dark and yet they sense that they are in a large space which leads into a basement. But it is too dark. They must go back to find some torch or matchsticks.

They come back into the main area of the repairing shop and search for some sort of light. The large door creaks and Isodore comes in with Henk. All three of the boys start to talk at the same time and all Isodore can see on their faces is excitement mixed with fear. They ask him to follow them and Henk follows behind. It is too dark inside and they leave the cave. Once again they are standing in the middle of the open space of the old shop. They close the large wooden door from the inside, so that nobody can get in.

Henk has a cigarette lighter in his pocket and he thinks he has seen some candles in the Chief's apartment. But they don't have so much time. So with the cigarette lighter they go in. And they are all flabbergasted. All those years that Isodore had been here, with his bicycle shop, he never could have imagined that there was such a huge space hidden behind his own shop!

But they mustn't tell the builders about this. Certainly Visigoth must not know any bit of it. It will remain a secret, their secret. So they all come out and try to look normal again. They stack the boxes in such a way that the broken wall is not visible anymore.

They have barely sat down when Visigoth arrives with the builders. Then the Chief also comes in with the Russian portrait painter Anatoly Manikin, who is actually an electrical engineer. He is a tall and very gentle guy with a friendly smile. Isodore looks at the Chief intently but says nothing. Visigoth looks at them and becoming suspicious, asks, 'What now? Is anything the matter? You dirty bunch are not trying to hide anything from me, are you?' The group remains silent.

At the end of the day, the builders' groups leave with Visigoth. Henk gets some ready-made noodles from an Indonesian fast food shop and they all sit down to eat first. Suddenly there is someone at the door. It is the Russian engineer and painter, Anatoly Manikin, who has forgotten to take his old jacket. He is very apologetic about entering the shop again so rudely. But they decide it is fine to add him to their secret group. After all he is an engineer from Russia. And is there any task that a Russian engineer cannot perform? In fact, is there anything on our planet that a very simple Russian is not capable of doing? The answer is simply a plain 'no'. Besides, he seems such a trustworthy fellow.

All of them go to move the boxes and make the passage empty. Soon they find a large door. A large backyard and large shed. Below that there is a hidden basement, where they could hide an entire world. The boys look at each other and their faces shine. Yes! The answer is there. There in that empty room, they are going to store all their boxes with bicycle parts. Perhaps later, when things get better, they will be able to get out the boxes and start a bicycle shop again, after all.

Only Visigoth will create problems. They all

think of that rude and choleric figure, who never lets anyone have any peace. Yes, he will do his best to ruin their discovery. They all go to sit down. The Russian painter and engineer Anatoly smiles and, sounding like a defence lawyer in a criminal case in court, says, 'Well, this place has always been your place, right? Imagine you have always used this place for safe keeping? Perhaps as a safe store room? Why should the others know about it?'

The three boys jump on him in happiness and clap their hands. 'Yes, Mr Manikin! We have always used this empty place as our hidden store room! Haven't we, guys? But it must have the look of an old and abandoned store room. It must look as if we have really used it! We can't allow Visigoth to be suspicious about anything. Oh that guy is a picture of ire itself.' Isodore smiles at the boys and says, 'Yeah, Visigoth has a sinecure job here. Like Mr Trump's job in the White House.'

Now they all laugh heartily.

Anatoly Manikin knows how to fix lights and soon there are lights inside the hidden space. There are brooms and buckets to use for cleaning! And before the night is over, that ancient space is clean and all the boxes are stored there as if they have always been there. They even find an old broken lock, which is hanging on a door, perhaps to go the basement.

'Perhaps we can use this lock on the other door so that the others will not be able to get in.'

Mongkut tries to take the lock off but he can't. Anatoly comes to help him. But the lock does not move. He checks the wall with his palm and a strange smile crosses his face. He looks at the Chief and says, 'We have to hide this wall, hurry up!' The Chief says, 'Well, the building costs are going to be higher than we thought.'

They come out of the hidden space before anybody knocks on the main door to get in.

The night does not have many hours left and they all want to rest.

'Shall we all go to your place, Chief?'

Henk has already got up with a bag in his hands and says, 'I have brought some clean towels for you.'

So they follow the Chief and go to the top floor. Henk has clean towels, an electric kettle and a pot of ground coffee. They can even take a shower and have a decent early breakfast in his place. 'You got a nice home, Chief. I'll see that you get a radiator too.'

Anatoly Manikin looks around to find some more spots that might need some attention to be fixed. He sounds like a domestic man who knows all about comfort.

Henk is the first one to wake up. He makes some coffee in paper cups and says, 'Hey Chief, you have got a grand place here. Except for those narrow stairs, one could live here forever. And you are not going to need so much room just for yourself? What I mean to say is, that, may I sometimes come here, just to stretch my legs a bit?'

The Chief does not say a word. Because he knows that from now on, he is going to have a permanent neighbour in his own tiny room. But he does not mind. He also shared his buffalo skin tent with many others, on that Mountain of Arizona, his grandfather's Mountains, where the sixth generation of Sitting Bulls were regular visitors. Besides, men should make space for their fellow men. Although we are now living in the Trumpian era, we just can't follow all his commands. That would not be nice to Trump's late mother either, who was a Scottish economic immigrant to the USA, from a little village on a small Scottish island.

Slowly they all wake up and feel their empty

stomachs. They run downstairs and to the new café. Visigoth must be there now, waiting for everyone and he must have some coffee and bread. As manager of the project, he must provide them with the necessary supplies. And sandwiches and coffee are at the top of the list.

Visigoth has indeed been waiting for them in front of the huge door and he is kicking everything around it. He could not get in because he did not have the key. Seeing them approach, he shouts at them, 'You ignorant cockroaches, what do you think you are doing here being so late? Are you only here to eat my bread? Drink my coffee? And you, the brown piece of a disgusting Indian, have I told you lately that I hate you? Why don't you just disappear and leave me in peace, hey? Why do I have to bring you your breakfast? And lunch? And dinner? Why me?'

None of them say a word as they go into the café. Visigoth's rage has not subsided and he goes on, 'I have lost everything that I had worked for. And you have got a café? I am the dupe of this situation, created by someone whose name I do not dare to utter! Now, how do you feel about it? Hey, answer me.'

No one says anything and he begins to kick everything around the shop. And one kick hits the hidden doorway!

The cardboard boxes collapse on to the floor and the doorway becomes visible. The surprise is too stunning for him and his mouth opens wide. He runs inside like a frenzied buffalo and looks at all of them as if he does not know how to ask a question. The Chief says to the boys, 'Now, boys, please take the rest of the rubbish into that store room for the time being. Later on, we'll have to take it all to Beren's farmhouse. Now, don't just stand there idly. Make your hands active and bring them here to help me.'

Visigoth looks at all of them with hatred and distrust.

'Store room? Ha, store room? Since when has Isodore had a store room behind this place? Hey, what is the trick?'

Just about then, Isodore comes in slowly. He can sense that something is not quite right. But before that, the Chief looks at his eyes sharply. He turns his back to Visigoth and says, 'Hey boss, good you are here so early. Visigoth is getting all upset about our store room behind this wall, which we have used for years now.'

Isodore mumbles and says, 'Yeah, our store room. And so what? You are like a lumbago, Visigoth. Why can't you just leave things alone?'

Then he looks at the three boys and says, 'Now, boys, I have asked permission for you guys from your guardians if you can stay here, under my supervision for the coming couple of nights.' Anatoly Manikin coughs to catch the attention of the Chief and sends him a winking message with his left eye.

The Chief says to Isodore, 'Now, Boss, I think it is better for the boys to sleep in their own camps. You see, too much freedom is not good for them. Besides, they were sent here to learn about fixing bikes. And we are now busy with something else.'

Isodore shakes his head as if he did not get the message and says, 'Now come and eat. Aaf baked bread in the morning. But Henk did not turn up to pick it up. So I had to come here.'

After many days, the three boys are not shy about the invitation from their boss. They jump on the bread and search for jam and sweet cookies. Isodore smiles at them and something like a prayer makes his chest calm. He looks at the boys again and wants to say something. But Faris opens up his full mouth first and says, 'Uncle Isodore, please tell Aunty Beren that next time, she should send some extra jam for me. See, I don't like my bread dry.'

Isodore has a large smile on his face. He looks at the other two boys and says, 'I'll tell your Aunty Beren that from now on, all of you must get extra butter and jam.'

'Yeah. Oh Uncle Iso! Thank you. Thank you, Uncle.'

The three boys are now dancing and pushing each other with happiness. Their Uncle Iso is thanking the Old Man above and with a deep sigh, he murmurs to himself, 'May I have a bit more time from *You* to see these three nephews of mine grow up into decent men?'

'The film is not done and the show must go on!'

19

The Dresden Piano

They all are gone home. Now the three asylum seeker boys reluctantly leave. They would rather be with their Uncle Iso. Or in the farm of Aunt Beren. Or staying overnight at the place of the Chief, which is tiny but very cosy. They have spent some time there and they felt very happy. The Chief has nothing but his presence to offer. And this friendly bunch of spontaneous acquaintances are more than happy to mark themselves as his guests. They feel a curious sort of honour to be called the friends of the Chief.

But it is the Chief who does not want them outside of their camps too much. Isodore does not get it either. His back has started aching. He puts the boys into his van and tells them he is going to drive them to their camps on his own. The sad boys are immediately cheered up and quickly go to sit in the back seat of his van. Immediately they start giggling and making jokes about the day's work. The main topic is of course Visigoth and they have voted unanimously that he is a buffoon and his skin is certainly made of buff.

Only the Chief and Anatoly Manikin remain in the shop. They look outside and check all the doorways. The builders will return early tomorrow morning. So they have got the whole night in their hands. They just can't share anything yet, with anyone. The whole day's hidden excitement is taking the form of reality now.

They open the store room door and go inside. Then they turn on the special builder's light and the whole place lights up, taking away the last bit of darkness. Anatoly goes to the wall, which they covered last time with cardboard boxes, and tries to feel the wall with his palms. He has an odd sense about it and shivers, not knowing the exact reason for it. Perhaps it is the bizarre situation that they are in.

Suddenly, the wall starts to move and a narrow door opens in front of them. The room is dark and they turn on their small army torchlight. But they feel on edge. They get so nervous and confused that they hold each other's hands. They are feeling the presence of some formless being around them, as if they are being watched by some incorporeal beings from far away. They look around and their eyes become wider and wider in suspense.

Where are they? This is a huge room which is so clean as if it was dusted a few minutes ago! There are gas lamps hanging on the wall, with beautifully decorated glass, probably from Venice. They try to light them and the gas lamps illuminate the whole room. The floor of the room is laid with expensive Italian marble. On top of that, a very expensive Persian rug runs from corner to corner. In the middle of the rug, a fairy-like figure in a vermillion velvet dress is dancing to frighten a bull! A huge bull, which is afraid of her brow beating!

There are objects looking like furniture, which are covered with large white cotton sheets! They take them off one by one. And the more they uncover them, the more confused they become. These are musical instruments from all over the world! Instruments from the East and West. A couple of Sitars and Tanpuras. A few sets of large and small Tablas. Some of them are made of brownish wood and some from metal. There are several pieces and sizes of Violins and Bamboo Flutes.

Some pairs of dancing bells with golden fastening strings, for use around the ankles of a classical dancer from South Asia, are lying on the floor, as if a dancer has just left them there! Anatoly picks up one set which contains at least one hundred small bells. A close look verifies to him that those bells are made of real twenty-carat gold! The bells feel warm in his hands, which gives him a sensation as if he can feel the dancer's warm breath around his neck. The smell of her rose perfume! What sort of dance had she been performing? Bharat Nattyam? Or Kaththak?

Some instruments are from India and Nepal. Some of them are European. Some of them they do not even recognise. Except for a piano, all instruments are there.

'Yes! A piano is missing from the list.'

The Chief is thinking, as if he can sense a clue to a huge mystery. Anatoly shakes his shoulder and says, 'Chief, this is a little orchestra! It is so clean as if someone has just finished performing a musical show!'

On the other side of the wall is a large man-size portrait of a sagely person. Seeing it, Anatoly murmurs his name, 'Tagore! Rabindranath Thakur! The Bengali poet. What is he doing here?'

'But how do you know who he is?' the Chief asks.

Anatoly looks at the Chief in a disappointed manner. For a moment he hesitates to answer him. But then he says, 'He was a Nobel Prize winner in the year 1913 for his literary works and is known worldwide. His works have been translated into almost every language. Both the old and young generations in Russia are crazy about his spiritual writings.'

Anatoly lets go a deep sigh, which sounds like, 'How on earth doesn't he know Tagore?'

They look at the other walls. Those too are full with oil paintings of famous pianists and musicians. Their names and date of birth and departure are written under their portraits. There are Bach, Beethoven, Mozart, Schubert, Handel, Vivaldi, Rachmaninoff and so on.

But what is the meaning of it? Who plays these instruments and who is keeping this place hidden from everyone's eyes? There must be a lot more to this than what is visible now. The Chief is completely speechless and does not even dare to touch anything. But Anatoly is searching for the solution to the mystery. He goes back to the life-size picture of Tagore and examines it.

Tagore is clothed in several layers of a long white cloak. His long white beard covers all his face and his long shiny grey hair is hanging down to his smooth neck. His two arms are crossed on his chest as if he is praying like Jesus used to do. His sharp nose and two large, dark, intelligent eyes are shining with wisdom. Anatoly looks at Tagore and it is as if he also smiles at him in return. He calls the Chief, 'Come here, Chief. Can you see anything unusual in this portrait?'

The Chief looks. But he sees nothing extraordinary. And he says, 'Anatoly, my head is spinning. Am I imaging things?'

Anatoly traces his fingers on the eyes of Tagore and he moves, as if he wants to step down from his frame! There is a hidden door behind the portrait of Tagore, which is locked from the other side. Anatoly pushes the door. But it does not move. He looks at Tagore and says, 'Now Guru-ji, keep watching. We'll see that you open this door for us some day. *Nomosker!*'

Slowly, the Guru-ji Tagore goes back to his own position automatically and stands there firmly as if to say, '*Nomosker* and don't disturb the peace!'

'Good day to you too, Guru-ji. Perhaps my grandfather knows you,' the Chief mumbles. 'You know the one, who lives on the top of the Arizona Mountains? Yeah, that is my grandpa. My father's father.'

They come back in utmost silence so that even a mouse would not feel disturbed. Now they are in the middle of the open space where Isodore used to have chains hanging from the ceiling to hang the broken bikes for repairing. They look around very carefully and detect no-one. Without turning on any lights, they leave the bicycle repair shop. They look around. No one is watching them. No police car is moving here. At this hour they are busy in the red-light area. And probably Visigoth is trying to keep up his business by exploiting the other girls.

Anatoly looks at the Chief in silence and they start walking side by side. They go up to the top floor of the Chief's apartment. The door is open and they go in. Henk is sleeping on the sofa-bed, covered by his only blanket. There is a small plastic table there now, with two tiers. A roll of toilet paper is standing on the lower tier and some empty used paper cups on the top. There is also a little worn out radiator. Probably Henk has found these things on the streets as usual. Anatoly looks at the radiator and checks it and says, 'It will do. I'll take care of it tomorrow morning.'

The Chief goes to sit in a corner of his room and tries to close his eyes. He must have been having very strange dreams. He wants to have a talk with his grandfather. He wants to ask him about that hidden place and the musical instruments. He wants ask him about that famous Sitar player, Ravi Shankar. How come his portrait is hanging in a hidden place like that? Is that all real? Perhaps he will go there alone tomorrow to check. But maybe all of it really is an illusion and tomorrow morning in broad daylight, all that magic will have vanished!

Morning can show the day. Morning can clear away confusions. But when he wakes up, he is even more confused. His room feels warm and cosy. The radiator is already installed and working. He has a little pillow under his head and he is covered nicely under his own blanket. The smell of coffee hits his nostrils and the sound of someone chewing hard bread makes him open his eyes.

'Good morning, Chief,' says Anatoly and Henk hands him a cup of coffee, saying, 'Thank you, Chief, for lending me your blanket. I'll find one soon for myself. But I must move now. Beren needs a helping hand.'

'We must also move, Chief, before Visigoth gets there.'

Anatoly heads to the staircase but the Chief calls him back.

'Please take the keys and tell Visigoth that I am taking a day off. I just need to clear my head, Anatoly.'

Anatoly smiles an understanding smile at him and says, 'Don't worry, Chief. Continue dreaming, till your dream turns into clear reality.'

Anatoly leaves and the Chief goes to lie down on his sofa-bed. His sofa has a rather strange smell nowadays. This place is becoming so alien to him. Too much comfort here, which has taken his old and known feelings away.

'They shouldn't have done it,' he thought and it seems that his grandfather agrees with him.

He moves from one side to another. Now that he is alone, he wants to talk to his grandfather. But since he has been sitting inside that golden frame, he has not talked much. Sometimes he does not even smile. He tries to think and finally he decides that it was all a horrible dream, a hallucination of some sort. He must get up and go to his work, before Visigoth gets there. And he must check the whole place before anyone meddles with things. He needs to clear up his visions for his own sake.

But the Chief is already too late. From the street, he can hear Visigoth shouting at the boys and they are shouting back at him in return. He enters the shop and finds the three boys around a huge wooden structure, which is covered with a sheet of oily plastic. He looks at it. That is the thing that made Posette faint! He recalls that event now very clearly. How frightened she was! But it was in the corner among piles of junks. Who has moved it to its present position? Yes, it is standing exactly covering the spot where they found a door last night!

He goes to have a closer look and the three boys try to speak at the same time, pointing at Visigoth. He looks at Visigoth and says, 'Stop this buffoonery, Visigoth. What seems to be your problem, man?'

Visigoth makes a fist and says, 'I want to open that plastic and I want to see what is under it. But these little foreigners, from who knows which parts of the slums, are not letting me go near to it! Why is that, may I ask?'

His loud breathing sounds like a dragon spewing fire through its nostrils.

The Chief feels alarmed and he looks at the three pairs of eyes of the boys. All he sees is confusion. That wooden structure has been moved to the wall where they had found the door. It looks as if someone has tried to push the wooden structure through that hidden door but failed. The wooden structure is too large to be pushed through that door. But where is that door! There is no sign of it. It looks like a bulwark of someone!

Anatoly comes in and seeing the Chief he wants to say something. The Chief looks into his eyes and makes a sign of confusion. Only Visigoth is shouting non-stop, 'And where is that door? Hey, where is that door of your hidden store room?'

The three boys shouts at equal volume, 'What store room? What hidden room? Hey Chief, did anyone ever see any door here?'

The Chief looks at Anatoly and says, 'Door? What door?'

Visigoth jumps up and down, screaming, 'You

dirty son of bitches. You dirty foreigners. Wait till our party wins the election. Then you will all be thrown out of all of our decent European countries. You plague! You bunch of tricksters.'

He spits on the floor loudly and goes to move the plastic off the wooden structure.

The three boys take up position around it on three different sides. The Chief moves near to Visigoth and says, 'Look, pal, this place belongs to Isodore till today. And everything that is inside this place belongs to him too. You may not touch or move anything without his permission. You may tell your labourers that too.'

Suddenly Isodore arrives with Henk, and Visigoth jumps to his feet again. But before he can open his mouth, Isodore begins, 'Not now, Visigoth. I am tired and besides, my three nephews are here with the Chief. Why don't you try to work together with them?'

'Your nephews? Those foreigners out of nowhere are your nephews? And you are asking me to work with this stinking brown Indian?'

Visigoth makes a fist again and Isodore says in an ice-cold voice, 'That is exactly what I mean?'

'You must be mad. These asylum seeker boys are

your nephews? That stupid Indian is your business partner now? Am I going mad?'

Visigoth runs outside in a rage.

Anatoly has been watching the whole scene in deep silence. Isodore looks at them questioningly and they all shrug their shoulders. No one has any answer to the mystery. What has happened to the door? And who has been trying to move that heavy wooden thing to the other side?'

Isodore indeed seems very tired. He says, 'Chief, what is that thing? Why did Posette faint, just seeing a bit of it? What are we going to do with that thing? Shall we ask Visigoth to remove this piece of rubbish and get rid of it?'

'No, no! We must not do that.' All of them answered in one voice.

'We will keep it the way it is. After the builders are gone, we'll open it in the presence of Posette. Perhaps she will have some answers for us.'

'Okay,' Isodore agrees with a very tired voice.

'But that Posette? Can you tell me why she behaves so strangely whenever she sees me? She just can't stand my voice! I find it all so odd.'

'Uncle Iso, please go home. We are here and we'll take care of everything.'

The three boys now go closer to him and take him by his hands.

'Let's bring you home, Uncle Iso.' Isodore looks up at the ceiling where the light is coming through and smiles at the boys.

'But what should I do, being alone at home?'

'Okay. Then you don't have to go home. Let's bring you to Chief's place. He has got a nice place and it is very close by. You can rest there and one of us will be there all the time with you. In that way, you'll not be alone and you can relax too.'

'Yeah, and at the end of the day, we'll bring you home. Okay, Uncle Iso?'

Isodore smiles at the boys and thinks, 'It is wonderful to have some nephews around!'

The boys do not bother to ask the Chief if they can really bring Isodore to his place. Perhaps that is the way things are done in their own culture. Friends share their friends' possessions whenever the need might arise.

Isodore meets Visigoth outside his huge wooden door, where he is standing and shouting to a worker. Perhaps Mecho has left him in charge of the work.

'Now, Visigoth, that thing that is covered with

plastic must remain there. We'll take care of it when Mecho's work is done. No one must touch it. And I'll be in Chief's place now. If you might need me, you know where to find me.'

Visigoth looks at Isodore with all the venom in his eyes and the three boys laugh at him.

'Yeah, Mr Visi, see that things are done properly here. We don't have much time. So don't be lazy, like the foreigners are. Ha ha.'

Their laughter is so contaminating that even Isodore has to smile with them.

These boys, who are full of compassion and energy, who call him their 'uncle', what is going to happen to them? Is there a way for him to help them? To make them his real relatives? The Old Man above has sent them to him. Why can't he keep them alongside him, as a true family?

'The film is not done and the show must go on!'

Ad fin

Absit Omen

Today is the 14th day of February, Valentine's Day. The day of love and for lovers. This day has been selected for the grand opening of the café. There has been no dilly-dallying with the work by Mecho. Exactly at the end of the sixth day of the renovation work, he handed over the key to Isodore. It was all done, clean and completely ready to open the doors.

For the opening, they will need some stools, chairs and tables and Mecho says that he will arrange all of that from IKEA. Mecho is a well-connected man and reliable as a rock. He knows how many cups and utensils will be needed in a café like this. And IKEA is the answer for everything. Mecho's group will also arrange everything for tomorrow's opening. So nothing can go wrong.

And what can go wrong? Behind the wall is a modern kitchen, equipped with everything that might be required. Mecho's men have taken a day off for tomorrow. They know how to run a café. They are Russians and running cafés for them is a piece of cake. As they say, a Russian uses all the cells of his brain. They are not lazy bums.

Isodore has talked with the guardians of the three boys and obtained permission for them to stay out one night, with him, and he'll thus be responsible for them. Anatoly and the Chief are checking the last bit of the electric works. All seems okay.

There is no big work to be done. The only thing they will do tomorrow morning is clean that wooden thing under the dirty plastic. They wanted to open it today. But Posette did not feel like coming all the way here, just to see something that she has no interest in. She did not talk with the Chief. And she is rather reluctant to talk with Isodore.

The only communication they have had with Posette is through Henk. And Henk has said that 'Posy' requested to tell them that she will certainly be here for the opening of the café. She had always hoped that someday she might be able to work in a café as a waitress. And now that the farm does not need so much work from her, she may be able to come and work in the café. Henk has already consented to give 'Posy' a lift twice a day. For an expert driver like him, it will be nothing to bring her to the café and return her safely to her home.

'I'll do anything for the comfort of 'Posy', you know.'

The Chief feels like punching his flat nose to make it bleed. Since when has his 'Pos' become a 'Posy' for idiots like Henk? His heart aches. But he says nothing. This is no time to fight. It is time to swallow pain and grief.

They look around again. All looks grand and new. The three boys have been told to be here early, because by nine o'clock in the morning, the van from IKEA will be coming to deliver the furniture and the rest of the equipment. Mecho has also built a dressing room next to the kitchen and behind that a medium-size bathroom and toilet for private use. The toilets for ladies and gents look ravishingly decorated. People can sit there and enjoy a long conversation with each other.

They all feel very light hearted, knowing that

they can go home and relax. They should sleep well and gain the physical energy for tomorrow. Even Anatoly wants to have a relaxed sleep in his own bed. The boys leave for their own home and Henk takes Isodore in his van to head for the farmhouse of Beren.

They all feel the need to be in their own dwellings tonight, the precious night before the grand opening. Instead of a formal shaking of hands, they all jerk each other's shoulders by gripping them in a warm and friendly gesture. They are all hoping for a smooth opening of their café tomorrow evening and all the days that follow afterwards.

But none of them feel any excitement inside their chests. It is as if nothing new or challenging is happening. As if everything is business as usual. The only thing is that they still have to clean something which is covered with dirty plastic. And maybe Posette will show up. Maybe she will want to have a job in the café as a waitress. But that too is for Isodore to decide. He has always been the boss here.

The Chief is walking towards his one-room apartment and now he is thinking about it. Nothing is very clear, though. The café is called

'Chief's Café'. But why? That place belongs to Isodore. Why did not they call it Isodore's Café? Or something else? How come he did not think about this before? After tomorrow, he'll certainly talk about it with Isodore. And Posette? Does she really want to work here, being in the close proximity of Visigoth, that egregious beast!

And again concerning Posette? He has not seen her for a long time now. She got married, had a child and is now a widow. What does she look like nowadays? And her baby boy? Why should she work in a café in the evening, leaving her baby alone at home?

In the meantime, he has reached his top-floor room. The door has been left open and he just goes inside. There is some food on the little plastic table, which feels warm. He does not feel like touching it. The face of Visigoth comes to his mind like a demon and that picture subdues the feelings of hunger. He goes to lie down on his sofa-bed and closes his eyes.

This room is not the same anymore. It was very different once. And then it was precious. Some precious beings were here to share the warmth of his soul.

Suddenly he starts to miss things again. How is that little gem of his? How is she doing in the ghost-house of that dark enchantress? Is she alive for that matter? Is she safe? He has no way to get near her. But he has also not tried. He could have tried it. Why did not he do that? He could do it now? Now that his room has got a toilet and shower? He could make a partition by hanging a curtain or something like that to divide up the room into two. Surely Aleppo would not mind?

But then he thinks about the reality. Aleppo or Amal or Lara is not safe from some unknown evil. Again the face of Visigoth flashes across his mind. Why does the Old Man above need to create things like Visigoth, by giving him a human form? Couldn't he give him a shape of what he really is? A Mephistopheles in human shape!

Someone is shaking him and several voices are calling him at the same time. He opens his eyes abruptly and feels shaken by suddenly seeing the three refugee boys in his room. For a moment he does not know where he is and how the boys got here. Even his room feels like an unknown place to him.

The boys are pulling him now and they are

saying things that are not very clear. He takes his leather jacket in his hands and runs down the staircase with them. The boys are shouting and telling him things. But nothing goes into his brain. He feels so sleepy and tired. He feels he must continue sleeping.

Faris knocks on the door and someone opens it from inside. It is Isodore, with a deadly look on his face. Now it is time to open his eyes but as soon as he has done so, he closes them again in a fit of panic. The suddenness of events takes his wits away. He looks around and looks again at the faces of the three boys and at the face of Isodore. All he can say is, 'Are we all dreaming!'

The whole place is shining like a golden temple! That piece of old dirty plastic is gone. In the corner of the room, a shiny wooden structure is standing. It is clean and its ancient wood is shining from the use of some expensive furniture oil. The brass wheels on its front legs are polished such a way that one can see one's face in them. It looks so grand and so special!

'Now, Chief, what is this thing?' Isodore's voice sounds so frightened.

'I don't know, Iso. It looks like a piano of some

kind!'

The boys scream at him and say, 'Let's open it, Chief. Let's see what is inside it.'

'No. We must wait for Anatoly. He'll know what to do.'

At this point they look around to see the inside decoration of their café. Their eyes are about to pop out of their sockets! They roll their eyes again and again. It is not a dream after all. The furniture that is there is not from IKEA. The boys stare and count the chairs. There are exactly ninety golden chairs, covered with soft crimson cushions. Each chair has got strings of small tables of mahogany. On the tables are gold rimmed decorated Slovenian wine glasses and Scottish crystal champagne glasses, all gleaming like diamond.

On the seat of each of the ninety chairs, a name is written in gold ink, on soft embossed turquoise paper, which smells like the roses of Shiraz. Ninety dark red roses have been put next to the names of those guests; each rose tied with gold ribbons. A message is written on the ribbon in rouge, which says 'LOVE'.

They try to read the names of their guests but none of the names are familiar to them. The chairs have been put around the room against the wall, so that there is a large open space on the floor. It is obvious that the guests will be able to view each other and to dance, if they feel like it.

There is also an envelope for Isodore. He does not dare to open it. The boys hate letters and the Chief has never received any letter in his life. They don't feel any curiosity about the letter, only the urge to know the instructions for the whole day. There are incessant questions in their confused minds. They must call someone.

These are the mobile communication days but none of them has a mobile phone in their pockets yet. They look around to find a device they can use to communicate. This place is lavishly decorated, with the most expensive objects that money can buy. There is even a huge ancient grandfather's clock, so large that one can hide inside it. But no phone!

They are looking at each other and hoping for a miracle to happen. Right at that moment, there is a knock on the new door and the boys want to run to open it. But Isodore makes a gesture and he goes to check who that is. The Russian builder has also fixed a secret eye-hole on the side of the door and also a hidden camera. He can see the nefarious face of Visigoth. First, he thinks he'd rather not open the door. But he does and closes the door behind him.

Visigoth wants to step inside and says, 'Aren't you letting me in? I want to see what is going on. What secrets are you thugs keeping from me?'

'Visigoth, we are busy now. You have done your bit of the job and got paid well. Please don't bother us anymore.'

Before Isodore can finish his words, Mongkut comes up and says, 'Uncle Iso, please tell that gonzo that he is not welcome here. Not even tonight.'

'Uncle Iso? That brown little thing is addressing a white man as 'uncle'? Am I going through a nightmare? Not even tonight? What is going to happen tonight? And why I am not welcome, may I ask?'

'You are just not welcome. It must be your egregious nature that makes you unwelcome to decent folks.'

The Chief is trying to dismiss Visigoth and in the meantime he sees Anatoly approaching. He feels relieved seeing this kind-natured fellow and says, 'Hey Anatoly, right on time. The coffee machine is not working. Please check the electrics again. We don't want to bother Mecho for such a triviality.'

Anatoly Manikin is a calm man who has his wits about him. He realises that something upsetting is going on inside and they don't want Visigoth to witness that. As soon as Anatoly has come in, the Chief closes the door and they can all hear Visigoth shouting and violently kicking the newly painted ancient wooden door, swearing in every language he knows.

Anatoly too is puzzled by the decorations. He looks at their faces and they all point to the letter that is lying on the big table. The letter is written in Dutch and Anatoly tries to take a clear message from it. The letter is obviously meant for Isodore, giving him instructions for tonight's grand opening.

For one thing, there will be a dress code. Everyone's dresses are kept in the dressing room, also for the ladies. There will be ninety guests altogether, many from the top level of society. They are business magnates, directors of the national and other important museums, top bosses of multinational companies, bank-directors, lawyers, diplomats, doctors, top police bosses, politicians, senior and top of the top judges, and of course the mayor of the grand city of Amsterdam.

They will sit on the chairs, which have labels with their names. No uninvited person may enter into the café tonight. The guests will arrive at half past ten and will first drink some Slovakian pink champagne and then some special South African wine, which will be served with unusual delicacies.

There will be a piano player, who will play the piano that is standing in the corner of the café. The guests may dance, if they feel like dancing. Finally, no reporters or journalists are allowed to be present at tonight's revelation!

Anatoly finishes his reading and looks at them all.

'Piano playing? Who is going to play the piano? And what sort of piano is that?'

The boys' mouths are wide open now. They all look at the Chief, who looks at Isodore and says, 'Isodore, recall what happened when Posette was here for the first time? She swooned on seeing the legs of that thing, which is called a piano. We must have her here tonight. I know that she had piano lessons as a child in her village. And secondly, we must try to figure out the mystery of that thing.'

Isodore seems very worried and says, 'But Chief, she can't stand me near her, even though I have never meant any harm or done anything that could hurt her feelings!'

Anatoly goes close to that wooden thing and wants to check it first. It is a certain sort of piano, no doubt. He opens the front cover of it. There is an inscription in gold saying, 'Jos.Kulb.Dresden.5742.'

That does not reveal much and it sounds phony.

'Let's open the top and see if the hydro-cell bar is there. We need to soak it before playing.'

Anatoly tries, while they are all watching him. But it is all in vain. He cannot open the top board of the piano. It is smoothly and tightly closed.

The Chief looks more thoughtful and says, 'Anatoly, do you realise that we have not arranged any bit of all this? Whoever the persons behind this are, they have cleaned this ancient piano and presumably made it ready for playing. But they have not tried to take it! If they had, they could have succeeded. Look at the chairs and the decorations! They are certainly not from IKEA! And Mecho did not order those for us.'

'No, he didn't. Because he was told to cancel the order from IKEA,' Anatoly says quietly. He is the only one who does not seem to be surprised by any of it.

The boys look around some more. They go to the dressing room but come out screaming. There are three packets of large suits and their names are written on them. And there are three pairs of shoes. They open the packets and their eyes become wider and wider in disbelief. Those are suits that the kings or presidents of their own country would never be able to wear! And those shoes? Isn't that something that they have seen before? Some guys coming to their place wearing these sorts of priceless suits and shoes? But who has brought these clothes for them?

'Uncle Iso, is this a dirty joke on us?'

All three of the boys look sad and scared now.

'No boys. It is no joke. We all have to wear these clothes tonight, which have been laid there in the dressing room. There must be packets for all of us.'

The boys run into the dressing room again and come back with some boxes. There is a simple black suit and pair of black shoes for Isodore. A suit for someone who is supposed to be the bar-man. A black velvet lacy dress for the lady pianist. A pair of half boots made of buffalo leather for the Chief.

The boys look at the Chief in dismay as if they want to ask him, 'Where is your packet of clothes, Chief?'

Perhaps he can read their minds and he says, 'I suppose the suit for the bar-man will fit you, Anatoly?'

'So no going home early tonight,' Anatoly murmurs.

'Let's examine the whole place first, starting with the kitchen and toilets. And of course the food. Alcohol alone is not going to make everyone happy. Delicious food is a must for nights like this. We must not fail that person or persons who arranged all of this for you, my dear Isodore.'

Now they hear some noise outside the main door and the Chief goes running to open the door. He spots Henk's van standing there. A lady, who is all covered with a shawl, is waiting to be let out. But Visigoth is blocking the door. He is shouting at Henk and it is as if fierce gunpowder balls are coming out of his mouth. Seeing the Chief, he becomes twice as irate, while Henk is saying to him, 'Yes, I can go in there in that new café, and so can this lady. You just have to understand that sometimes two plus two is not four, but five.'

'Ooch. Is that so?' Visigoth shouts.

The lady comes in and she removes the shawl from her head. They all look at her. But she does not greet anybody. Instead she looks around and goes over to the piano. There are two stools there. One is a single one, with a crimson red cushion and gold plated ribbons around it. The other one is a two-seater. It is made of very fine oak and a beautifully decorated green velvet seat covers the box, which contains lots of music scores, written on something like sheepskins.

Perhaps it is meant for the use of duet players. But three could sit on it comfortably.

Posette opens the lid of the single stool and takes out some music scores from the inside box. The music is written by hand on very old paper. She looks at them and her hands tremble. Then she strikes one note and suddenly she produces a loud scream, 'Isidore, let me go!' She has fallen into a swoon, perhaps by the frisson of excitement.

The boys take her into the back dressing room and someone gives her a glass of water. All the time, the Chief has been watching her. She did not even look at him or even say a simple 'hello', as if she had no recollection of him! And she looks so different now. Of course she is the mother of a little boy and a widow now. But how could she not say a word to him? And why is she so afraid of that generous and kind man Isodore? Why did she come here anyway?

'The film is done–'

The Tyros
Cherchez La Femme

The huge grandfather clock strikes exactly at ten in the evening and the boys are standing ready by the door inside. They have also been given three expensive modern iPhones, which they have found in their suits' pockets. They have no idea how the phones work. The SIMs have been placed inside and there is enough credit to make a call. They try to call each other. But that is not a great success. However, at this moment, they are happy that they can check the exact time on their mobile phones.

There are some other guys standing outside in shiny uniforms. Their job is to check the invitation letters of the guests and let them in. They are large and robust guys and it is obvious that they are guards provided by Mecho.

Isodore is standing awkwardly in a corner with

a wine glass in his hand. The Chief is standing next to the piano, where several other stools are placed. He feels his legs and wants to sit down. But seeing the decoration of the stools he says to himself, 'Better not spoil things. These stools must be meant for some very special guests.'

It is dark outside. The clock strikes half past ten and one by one, the guests start to come. They all find their seats but they try to avoid each other's eyes. Suddenly there is an uproar and a guard comes rushing in to catch a stout guy who is running in front of him.

The stout guy goes directly to Isodore and, offering him a hand to shake, he introduces himself, 'Ucles Cristofori is the name. A descendant of the great Bertolomeo Cristofori of Florence. And even before him and before him, backwards. Finally we meet Isidore de Seville! I am the journalist who made a couple of appointments with you. But we never had the chance to meet. By the way, where is that lady? Isn't that Polish lady going to perform tonight?'

The guard catches him by the neck and tries to throw him out. The Chief says, 'No reporters are allowed here tonight. Why don't you come some other time?'

Ucles shouts at him and says, 'I know who you are. Don't you even dare to touch that piano! It belongs to me. Do you all hear me? I am the heir of that piano and I have come here to collect it.'

In the meantime another guard has come and the two of them throw him out on the street. He falls down near the feet of Visigoth, who has been standing on the other side of the road, watching the arrival of the guests. He looks at Ucles and says, 'Visigoth Wamba is the name, buddy. Stay here with me. Some known faces may turn up and we'll try our luck.'

But the huge wooden main door has been locked from outside as well as from inside now. Suddenly the streetslights go out and some sleepy and tired looking figures in strangely styled clothes approach the main door requiring access. Inside the large room the light has turned dim. The door opens to receive these particular guests. The door-man inside is calling out their names one by one, to announce their presence to the audience.

Mr Johann Sebastian Bach. A chubby-looking elderly man steps in. He shakes off his beautifully plaited off-white wig. His face looks red, set off against his white shirt and black tail-coat. In one hand, he is holding a scroll of music and in the other hand, a white silken handkerchief can be seen. His plummy reddish face shows the signs of him having a severe cold. Mr Bach looks around and says, 'Where is she? I have composed something new for her.'

Breno Morales shows Mr Bach his golden stool and he sits down with some discomfort.

The next guest is announced as Mr Sergei Vasilievich Rachmaninoff. This very serious-looking Russian detects Anatoly Manikin's presence in seconds and says something to him in an incomprehensible language. Mr Bach asks Faris, 'What is he saying?'

Faris looks at Anatoly and brings his mouth close to the ear of Mr Bach.

'He is asking how his great-great-great grandmother is doing.'

But in his other ear, Mongkut says, 'No, Mr Bach. He is saying that he started composing at the age of four and graduated from the Moscow Conservatory. Above all, he is Russian. How come his name was not first on the guest list for this evening's event? A Russian is in no way less than a

German. He has taken it as a serious offence in the name of the new tsar Putin the Great!'

Mr Ludwig von Beethoven. The door-man calls the name and a middle-aged guy enters in the room. He is wearing a long grey coat. His silver hair is thick and uncombed. His white collar is covered with a brilliant orange scarf. He has a vague look on his face and it seems he is sad. With an ear horn in his hand, he goes to sit on a stool near the piano. He does not talk or greet anyone either. They all feel a little discomfort and confusion about the situation now.

The door-man has to cough several times to clear his throat, to avoid any mistakes in pronouncing the name of the next guest. Now he calls the name of Mr. Johann Chrysostom Wolfgang Amadeus Mozart, who was baptised as Johannes Chrysostomus Wolfgang Theophilus Mozart, but is known to his audiences as Wolfgang Amadeus Mozart.

This young good-looking guy is dressed in a bright red tailcoat. The beautifully curved golden buttons of his red coat are open. A white silk scarf is keeping his neck covered. His thick hair is brushed back and pulled up in the elegant style of a chignon.

He is full of joy and looks around gleefully. They all look at him with pleasant surprise and greet him delicately, 'Hello! Amadeus. Late as usual. Having troubles with the ladies?'

In the meantime the door-man is calling another name. Mr Franz Peter Schubert. Amadeus turns to this small tubby man, who is not even five feet tall.

'Hallo Schammerl! Long time no see. How is the cough nowadays? Is Nanerl okay?'

Amadeus wants to hug this little man, who moves backwards and looks for a comfortable stool to sit on.

Franz is wearing a long brown coat. A thick black scarf is hanging from his neck. His round gold-rimmed glasses seem foggy inside. It must be from his steamy coughing.

'Come on, little mushroom, sit next to me.'

Amadeus points at a seat next to him and the little mushroom goes to sit there, with much discomfort. Obviously his cough is bothering him.

'I thought, a lot of dancing would be going on by now! But where is he?'

Franz looks around questioningly. The door-man announces the name of someone they have been waiting for.

'Mr Antonio Lucio Vivaldi!'

The young and jubilant Italian Antonio makes a jovial entry. He has brought his violin with him and starts to play and sing in Spanish!

'Que sera sera! Whatever is going to happen is now happening! Que sera sera!'

Antonio's white and high wig looks like a Turkish turban. His white silk shirt is almost covered by a red robe like a long cloth. He is the best among all the Baroque musicians but he never feels arrogant about it. In a sociable mood, he looks around and says, 'Now, who is playing the piano?'

'And who is dancing with your violin?' Amadeus butts into Antonio's query.

'Well, I just can't sit and wait till someone tells me something about something? My fingers are becoming jammed by now.' Amadeus puts his ten fingers together to squeeze and shakes them. He is clearly in a jumpy mood and goes to sit on the double piano stool. Immediately Sergei sits down next to him. Franz goes to sit on the other side and Amadeus screams, 'Schammerl, little mushroom, I am being crushed between the two of you.'

'Don't you boys dare to touch my music box!'

They all turn back and all of them stand up,

to make a bow to the figure that has just entered. Even Mr Bach makes a courtesy by bending his body, his left hand behind his back and holding a piece of music score in his stretched out right hand. Looking at the ground, he says with utmost respect, 'My queen, I have composed a new piece for you!'

The lady in the black velvet dress does not pay any heed to Mr Bach, or to anyone else for that matter. All of them are keeping their heads bent down. Her neck and shoulders are bare. A stud diamond necklace is coiled around her neck and there are two white diamond bracelets on her wrists. She is shining like sophistication itself.

But her dress! They have seen it before. Isn't it the dress that the late Princess Diana had on when she was dancing at the White House with John Travolta, having been invited by the Reagans? And that jewellery? And her silver shoes? A black piece of lace veil is thrown over her head, which covers her face down to her chest.

She moves close to Isodore and makes a bow to him, as if a queen is making a bow to her king! Then she turns to the others.

'Berenguela!'

A flabbergasted Isodore runs to Breno Morales and asks him to call the farmhouse immediately. A sleepy voice picks up the phone at the other end.

'Hallo, Aaf. It's me, Iso. Where are you?'

'Where I always am, sleeping on the floor of Beren's bedroom.' He hears a deep yawning and asks one more question, 'And where is the baby? Ivan?'

'Where he always is. On the chest of Berenguela. Now they are both sleeping on their bed. If you don't mind, I am going back to sleep too. Tomorrow is a heavy day for us.'

She hangs up.

Breno redials.

'Hallo. Hallo Aaf, are you sure that–'

The connection is broken off. Breno tries to redial her again but the mobile phone seems completely disconnected by now. Mongkut and Faris try their phones too. But all are dead. They look at Berenguela and clasp each other's hands and ask, 'Uncle Iso, that is not Aunt Berenguela, right?'

Isodore sits down on a chair and says, 'Frankly I don't know, boys. My head is spinning.'

Berenguela sits down on the single crimson

stool now and touches the keys with her long and slender fingers. Mr Bach stands up but then sits down again on his stool. He says a few words like, 'Yeah that piano. I played on it at the court of Dresden in 1733. I hope you all recall that Mass at the court and the piece, 'Kyrie and Gloria'!'

But none of them makes any response to his statement, as if they all are waiting for a command from the black-veiled lady.

Antonio stands up and accompanies her playing on his violin. Baroque-style music fills the room. The ninety guests cannot hold their feet tight together. It is as if their feet want to dance to this unknown divine music.

Suddenly the light goes out for a fraction of a second. And it comes back on at the same speed. On the floor two figures are dancing now. Both of the figures have their faces covered by gold masks. Only their eyes are shining inside the masks, like the burning eyes of hungry cheetahs. One is a lady in a turquoise velvet dress. A large pink stud diamond ring is shining on her finger. A large necklace of ruby and stud diamonds is lying lazily around her smooth and unusually beautiful curved neck. And her extra-ordinary turquoise-coloured shoes! One moment, it seems she is rather bulky and the next moment she looks very thin. How old is she? It is so difficult to guess. She is ageless.

'But that ring on her finger! Isn't that the ring from Lady Imelda Marcos?'

'Yes! And that necklace, for that matter?' One of the bank directors is whispering to a police boss. But no one is in the mood for this sort of gossip now. They are watching the two dancing figures, dancing hand in hand, intensely, as if a snake charmer is making his cobras dance, enchanting the audience.

But it is not her! It is the person with her that has taken away the breath of the ninety guests. It is a child. A unisex person! Its hair is tied up in a knot on top of its head. It is wearing white chiffon leggings and a white long-sleeved silk shirt. But it is about its turquoise dress! The dress is hanging just above its knees and resembles the kind of dancing dress that Turkish dancing boys would wear on a special dance evening for their sultan! The dress is round and it envelops around when the dancing child moves.

Two thin gold bracelets are hanging from her thin wrists. Gold dancing bells are hanging from her ankles, just above her ballet-like golden shoes.

The two figures are dancing and dancing away while Antonio is playing his violin and Berenguela finally gets Mr Bach to sit next to her.

The guests are watching the two dancers in amazement. That thin little dancer? Sometimes it looks like a boy. But when it turns around, it looks like a vulnerable little girl in her early teens. Are they real? The little dancer looks as if it is carved from a piece of turquoise stone created in the azure heavens and the generous heavens wanted to share a piece of that glory with the humans of the earth!

The little dancer could be a talisman for the turban of Solomon. Or for a Shaman's temple, on the top of the Tibetan mountains. Or it could protect the warrior king Saladin. Or it could be a protective talisman for the emperor of the emperors, like the Sultan *Muhtesem* Suleiman the Magnificent of the Ottoman dynasty!

The dancing child resembles a talisman of protection, which is made of opaque stone that is strong and at the same time soothing for the eyes, as if it is healing hearts that have been made dirty by greed! It moves around to the violin of Antonio and its skirt envelops its tender body. One of the guests whispers, 'It is called a 'wikkel-rok' in

Dutch. I have seen it in the deserts of Sub-Saharan Morocco, where Bedouin boys dance in it!'

Is this a human child? Or has it slipped to earth from the heavens by mistake, made by some jealous Gods! The dancing lady is holding one hand of the child tightly in her grip, as if the child could run away from her hands. They are dancing hand in hand. What is more enchanting here? The two dancers? The piano music of Berenguela? Or the violin of Vivaldi? They are dancing and dancing away. None of the guests has ever seen such a performance before.

Suddenly the child makes a move and separates itself from the hands of the lady dancer. It runs to the Chief, who has been watching the show standing in a corner, aloof from the others, his dark brown hat covering half of his face. His feet are hurting from wearing the new boots and his old leather jacket is stinking as usual. So to avoid being a public nuisance, he has kept himself apart from the guests, who are all smelling sweetly from their perfumes and very expensive aftershaves.

The little dancing figure runs to the Chief and holds him tight with its two thin arms and whispers, 'The film is done and the show...!'

Suddenly it is pushed backwards by someone. The Chief has a mysterious smile on his thin lips. He has received an answer to his prayers.

'Thanks, Grandfather!' he whispers. 'I'll sleep tonight after many nights! Thank you, heavens!'

The clock shows the time, exactly two minutes to three in the morning and the lights go off, creating a horrific dark inside the café. Immediately, the lights come on again. They all look at each other in disbelief. Their minds are still wondering, as if they are stuck in an enchanted forest.

By now a white ray of light illuminates the whole room. They all are still wandering in a dreamland. They don't dare to make eye contact with each other, because of the fear of losing it all. The musicians and the dancers have disappeared. The scent of Isfahani rose perfume is still lingering around the dancing floor. The rich and famous and most powerful guests have left one by one.

Their cars were waiting outside. Who could ever have guessed that this city has so many expensive cars, like Mercedes, Jaguar and Rolls Royce? Could a normal salary ever pay for those vehicles?

They didn't even notice that Henk left with Posette a long while ago. Iso, the Chief and the three boys walk hand in hand now, as if they all are sleep-walking in a wilderness. But now the Chief feels that they have a destination, that they are not lost, that they must go home. To his home. Because they all have to wake up tomorrow morning, on time. There will be a loads of work to do.

The café has to be cleaned and has to be open from now on for ordinary and everyday people. It will be a café for non-smokers and for families who have not got much to spend to go out and sit somewhere for a tea or coffee. It will be for those moms who earn just enough to pay the household bills. Or for those loving parents who want to give their children a sense of financial comfort, by showing that they are able to pay for a piece of cake, when they are sitting in a calm and warm, friendly place called 'Chief's Café, Amsterdam'!

' – And the show must go on.'

The wrath of Ucles
Chief's Café, Amsterdam, part II

The very next day, they are all there in the café. There is no sign of anything from last night. Perhaps it was not real. Instead of golden chairs, there are simple stools and chairs from IKEA standing there, next to simple, smallish tables, made of fake wood-like material. Just a normal café. They shake the bad dream out of their minds.

Suddenly, Ucles appears at the door of the café, with an interim order from the court. He claims he is the real owner of that Dresden piano. And nobody may play the piano or even touch it, until a final verdict is given by the court. Especially, under no circumstances, must anyone soak the hydro-cell bar that is hanging inside the piano. He also talks about the Etymology of Isidore de Seville. Anyway, he needs that hydro-cell bar! But why?

Dalir shows up, looking upset. The reason he is sad is not because he was not invited last night. It is that he is being stalked by one of his patients. This rather young man, called Sherkhanzai, believes that Dalir knows the whereabouts of his stolen wife, who is merely a child! This Sherkhanzai is in his early youth and it seems he really does not realise the difference between living on top of an Afghan mountain or in a city that is eight metres below sea-level! Besides, what does the son of a lion anticipate to get from him?

About the Author

Mithun B. Nasrin

The author is a teacher by profession. In her free time she loves to paint and sing. She has an MA and MSc from the University of Amsterdam and an MA from the University of Leiden, both in the Netherlands. Her previous works include novels, children's books, volumes of poetry and a language book published by Routledge. Her recent novel 'The Smell of Home' was published by Austin Macauley in London.

Her life is very much influenced by her father, who was a Sufi singer/composer, and her artist mother.

In her daily life, she follows the Sufi path of Omar Khayyam, the Persian Sufi mystic, poet and philosopher. She is currently researching the history of Sufi music in Spain.

This Dutch writer lives in Newcastle upon Tyne in the UK and has made South Gosforth her home.